Decision over Janos

Books in Starship– Cosmic Mall

The Earth's Project

Starship–Cosmic Mall

Decision over Janos

D. A. Tuskey

LANIER
PRESS

Alpharetta, Georgia

ISBN: 978-1-6653-0731-4 - Paperback
eISBN: 978-1-6653-0732-1 - eBook

These ISBNs are the property of Lanier Press (a Division of BookLogix) for the express purpose of sales and distribution of this title. The content of this book is the property of the copyright holder only. BookLogix does not hold any ownership of the content of this book and is not liable in any way for the materials contained within. The views and opinions expressed in this book are the property of the Author/Copyright holder, and do not necessarily reflect those of Lanier Press/BookLogix.

∞This paper meets the requirements of ANSI/NISO Z39.48-1992 (Permanence of Paper)

Original drawing of the *Cosmic Mall* starship by Jonathan Carpenter. Cover concept artwork by Kevin Bingham.

101823

*She's still my strongest supporter and since this book is a
continuation of the first,
To my wonderful wife,
Sarah.*
Thank you, My Love.

CHAPTER ONE

FINDING MORE CLUES

The group of three males and one female sat in a dimly lit room in a pub on Janos. They had each gotten there separately. The one male who appeared to be the leader spoke in a low but confident voice to the female, "I hope your information concerning Salfrod is accurate. With the way you botched your initial meeting with him, I'm not sure you're the right person for this job."

She squirmed nervously in her chair but, then, collected herself and said, "If your people had thoroughly briefed him on the sabotage, he wouldn't have reacted as he did. Besides, he wouldn't have been there in the first place since, it appears, he wasn't fully in agreement with the purpose of the plot. Whoever recruited Salfrod was less than diligent. In fact, they were inept!"

The leader replied, "The person responsible for Salfrod's recruitment has been dealt with. Suffice it to say he won't be doing any more recruiting." He paused, then continued, "Or much of anything else."

The others grinned, enjoying the intent of the unspoken statement. After a minute of savoring the taste of their preferred beverages, the leader spoke again, "If any of you think that I am inept, I'll remind you how successful our conspiracy was. And it could have been even more so had the actions of our agent on board the *Mall* starship not delayed our plan several weeks. I wonder who was the more inept." He now directed a piercing stare at the female, who cringed at the implication of such a malevolent look.

She spoke hesitantly. "I gave my complete cooperation to these other two you sent to sabotage the A deck. Without my help, they couldn't have gained access to the control room."

"And it's for that reason that I am allowing you to remain as our agent on board the *Mall* ship. But don't be too relieved. I won't tolerate another mistake. Having said that, I have another assignment for you."

The meeting continued for another hour. It ended with the leader saying to the other two males, "I haven't commended you two on the way you spirited Ambassador Calluran out of the A deck and transported him over to the *Hawk*. He is now ensconced safely here on Janos. He has served his purpose in our plot but may still be useful in the future."

One of the two males said, "The *Mall* ship has not been recalled and their mission might still be continued. Do you have an idea concerning how you might counteract that?"

The leader answered with malicious intent.

"Oh, I have a plan for that. And let me tell you, any

attempt the officers on the starship *Cosmic Mall* make, they will greatly regret it. I promise you!"

A full week had passed since the A deck sabotage had occurred and the investigative team on board the starship *Cosmic Mall* was busy trying to piece together the little information they had been able to uncover concerning the tampering done to the locking mechanism on the door to the A deck control room and the complete dismantling of the fail-safe.

The investigative team consisted of most of the command staff for the *Mall* starship. The leader of the team was ship captain Keanyn Mathews, second-in-command Grannison Loche, and science officer MacCardle Stinson.

Others who were major contributors were head of security Robert Porter, his assistant Ross Carter—who was currently busy making sure the huge shopping venue that was the *Cosmic Mall* was safe—undercover operatives ND and her son, Stenn, and Lieutenant Cheng Wong who had oversite of the immense shuttle deck on the ship.

The sabotage previously mentioned had occurred when the fail-safe mechanism that controlled the very unique feature called the A deck malfunctioned and allowed the, purely, atmospheric walls of the deck to retract. The happy outcome that resulted from the quick-witted thinking of Stenn that saved his life and the lives of four others, including Mac and Edward, Grannison's half brother, had softened the blow they all felt from the loss of some six hundred lives in the vacuum of space when the atmospheric walls had suddenly been lowered.

Another factor that kept the disaster from becoming an especially tragic event had been the determined actions of

ND. She had run into the A deck in an effort to collect as many of the children as she could with the added hope of getting their parents as well. She succeeded in saving the fifteen children and, either one or both parents of six of the children.

They knew that someone was still on board acting as an undercover operative for the one who was masterminding the plot against the Earth's project. Ambassador Yahnsoof Calluran, the diplomatic liaison for those visiting the starship *Cosmic Mall*, was missing and at the head of the list of those they suspected.

These were the thoughts that occupied the minds of those on the investigative team. But there was one other issue on the mind of, at least, one of the team, and it involved Edward's narrow escape with Stenn and all the questions he had asked.

Grannison had already anticipated Edward's curiosity. When their investigative group met that evening, he asked the others if he could include Edward in their clue-gathering team.

Most felt it was a good idea, seeing how the two half brothers were so close and how, especially after the A deck disaster, Grannison would be very hard-pressed to keep the information a secret. The exceptions to the approval were, as might be expected, Robert Porter and ND.

"It's not a matter of trusting Edward that concerns me," noted Robert. "It's just the delicate nature of our investigations. Can the security of our inquiries be maintained if we add more people to the mix?"

ND chimed in, "That was my thought as well. Too many people knowing about our investigation and the information we've uncovered makes the risk of a leak more possible."

It was Stenn who came to Edward's defense. "I would have felt exactly the same as you two if I hadn't spent those days in close company with Edward." As he said this, he turned his gaze on Grannison and said, "You have a very smart brother there, commander. I mean, we all knew of Edward's intelligence and skills, but, except for his brother, none of us appreciated his shrewd mind and powers of observation. He was closely questioning me the whole time we were in sick bay and even when we rested while in the A deck storage compartment. He had a pretty good grasp of what we were up to."

"That's why I asked if we could include him." stated Grannison, adding, "Some of you may remember the story I told you about taking Edward with me when I made that run to the moon to investigate the repeated vandalism perpetrated on the 'Moonberry' harvesting station." As he recounted the incident, the pride he felt for Edward was seen in his eyes.

Robert said, "Then why didn't we include Edward when we first created this investigative committee?" He then added with a wink toward the rest of the group, "In fact, we probably should have left out Grannison instead!"

From the midst of the chuckles, Grannison's voice boomed, "Well, I suppose if we were going to include a security officer who can't make a move without the consent of his surrogate mother and brother, we could include a pilot who had been relied upon by the Galactic Legion to run several undercover investigative missions."

This comment was not taken lightly by Robert, who retaliated with, "I don't need to prove my skills to anyone. I don't deny the excellent training I received from ND and Stenn, but I am not dependent upon their approval for any course of action I take."

Grannison, realizing that his comeback to Robert's harmless dig was a bit over the top, stood up and looked directly at Robert saying, "Of course I am fully aware of your credentials and accomplishments and I know you can succeed without their aid. But I don't appreciate it when someone suggests that I am not qualified either! I realize your comment was made in jest, but it wasn't funny to me!"

The rest of those in the room were completely quiet and motionless as Robert began to speak, "Commander Loch, I believe the added stress we have all been under recently has made us more sensitive than we might otherwise be. I spoke out of turn and I apologize. We've got more important things to attend to."

Grannison visibly relaxed and mustered up a grin as he said, "Your point is well taken and I agree. We've got no time for petty differences. Apology accepted—that is, if you will accept mine. Now let's get on to the important things!"

Captain Mathews got the discussion back on track. "I think it is now safe to say that Edward will be a positive addition to our investigative brain trust. We need to get on with our next plan of action."

All of them agreed this time and Grannison used his comm unit to call his half brother to their secluded corner of the officers' mess. When Edward arrived, they filled him in on the purpose of their conclave and what clues and other information they had previously gathered.

He said, "I already had my own thoughts on the matter and most of them agreed with yours, but as for the stowaway, I had been questioning Dr. Karushkin—the *Mall* Ship's head physician—off and on and had some knowledge of Salfrod's status. I'm glad he's turned the corner and is willing to help. As for Ambassador Calluran, I can't say I suspected him but I thought his behavior of late was odd."

"What do you mean by odd?" queried Stenn.

"Well," said Edward. "I almost bumped into him coming out of the shuttle deck into the mall anteroom about two weeks ago and he barely acknowledged me when I excused myself. I heard him muttering under his breath about ungrateful relations who never appreciated anything you did for them. I've never known the ambassador to be vocal about his family situation." After pausing, he continued, "In fact, I didn't know he had family alive."

Keanyn brought Edward up to date with the comment, "He doesn't have much family still around, apart from his sister's son, Ansmed, who, by the way, was the pilot of the ship our good Salfrod transferred to this ship from."

Edward reacted to this with a wide-eyed stare and an open mouth, but recovered and motioned for Keanyn to continue, which he did. "The ambassador's sister went missing some five years ago and has never resurfaced. Ansmed had been released from prison a couple of years earlier for his involvement in raider activity against our supply ships during the early days of the Legion's involvement with Earth. They conducted a pretty exhaustive investigation into his possible involvement in his mother's disappearance but couldn't find any connection. He appears to have been a model citizen from then until this incident involving our stowaway."

Robert Porter, who had been closely taking in this discussion between the captain, Keanyn, and Edward, now spoke up. "I've been trying to figure out Edward's comment concerning his recent contact with Ambassador Calluran and that muttered statement about ungrateful relations. Your mention of Ansmed has triggered a thought."

"What might that be?" Mac asked. "I've learned that

any thought you might have usually has a good bit of substance to it."

"Thank you, Mac," stated Robert with a smile toward the science officer. "I was wondering if the enigmatic comment by the ambassador might refer to his nephew, Ansmed, and some real or perceived action on his part that was felt, by the ambassador, to be either ungrateful or even traitorous. If it's the former, then it is at least curious. If it's the latter then a possible clue to the involvement of them in the sabotage plot."

Grannison injected his thought. "Are you saying the ambassador and his nephew may have had a falling out because of a difference each had in carrying out the sabotage plot?"

"That, or they simply had an argument where Ansmed displayed disrespect to his uncle. In either case, it shows that Ambassador Calluran has had recent contact with our stowaway's captain," finished Stenn.

"Let's not jump to conclusions," said Keanyn. "While I agree that those two assumptions have a lot of credence, they are still assumptions. Until we can get some concrete evidence that the ambassador is involved in the sabotage plot, we are only guessing based on circumstantial evidence."

Stenn spoke next and there was an air of apology in his words. "You're right, captain. I should have qualified my statement as an educated guess. I am just so anxious to get this investigation solved, I'm losing my objectivity. I want this project to succeed so badly, I lost sight of the main rule of an investigation."

His mother, ND softly interrupted, "And that is to keep your options open."

Mac had been holding back from commenting, wanting to hear from the "experts" first. She decided that now was the time to speak up. With a brush back of her hair as she adjusted her posture, she got everyone's attention. "I've been wondering about that incident concerning the last known sighting of Ambassador Calluran. Has anyone followed up on him being seen going into the Raushdonian pub, The Frothy Mug?"

Grannison said, "With the release of Edward and you other two from sick bay, my mind has been divided. However, I did look into it to a degree and discovered that the ambassador had gone into the pub under some amount of coercion from his two escorts who were possibly crewmen from the *Hawk*, his nephew's ship."

"And just how did they get on this ship without our noticing them?" inquired Robert incredulously.

It was Stenn who offered an explanation, but this time it was in the form of a qualified guess along with a wink and a nod to the captain. "My guess would be that they came aboard with the entourage from Janos, posing as minor dignitaries."

"But how could they have gotten past our guards when they came aboard?" asked Keanyn. "We were very careful to double-check everyone disembarking from the shuttles!"

Stenn continued with his theory. "I would suspect they forged their papers before coming aboard and, probably, picked two individuals from Janos who were locally appointed officials from a very small district on the planet, not well known by other dignitaries there. They would most certainly have either done away with the real officials or gotten them out of the way by some means that didn't arouse much suspicion."

Robert answered the hypothesis by saying, "That is very possible but shows us a glaring flaw in our security."

"I agree with you, commander," noted Keanyn. "We

seem to have a blind spot in that area. First, a stowaway with instructions to sabotage the ship gets aboard undetected, and, now, two others have boarded this ship without our knowledge. Add to that Ambassador Calluran's disappearance and we've got a serious breach in security! What do you propose to do about it?"

Robert did not back down from the rebuke but noted, "I should have made room for advanced technology, captain. I am solely to blame. But, I believe that is the problem. The *Hawk* must be equipped with an advanced form of transporting that our equipment can't detect. I won't rest until we get to the bottom of it!"

At this point, Lieutenant Cheng Wong expressed a thought. "I don't know about the rest of you but I've been trying to figure out when our enemies were going to make a second attempt at sabotaging this vessel after their first one with Salfrod was derailed. Now that we have the unfortunate answer to that question, the next one is how they were going to do it. I think we might have the answer in these two crewmen from the *Hawk* seen escorting Ambassador Calluran into the Frothy Mug."

Stenn broke in saying, "I think I know where you're headed, lieutenant, but would you mind clarifying?"

Cheng continued, "The two *Hawk* crewmen were, probably, computer specialists sent to disable the fail-safe for the A deck as well as to jam the lock for the door into the control room."

Mac, who was beginning to get Cheng's train of thought, said, "And it must have taken them until our fourth port of call to bring those two up to speed on their plan."

"That and they didn't want to try immediately after our first planetary stop in order to give us a false sense of security," chimed in Edward with the agreement of several others.

Grannison remarked, "That strategy seemed to work." As he said this, he noticed scowls form on the faces of several in the room. He quickly changed his tone of voice and continued, "We did become lax at checking the incoming dignitaries, leaving most of that to be done by the security personnel on the planet. Obviously, that has to change."

ND expressed her thoughts firmly, saying, "As Robert has already expressed, I can assure you that, and many other things, will be reexamined and changed if we find any of our security operations or operatives need the slightest tweak. In fact, I think now would be a good time for Robert to update us on what he has discovered in his scrutiny of the Raushdonian pub's owner."

Robert thanked ND and explained, "Hammfrual, the owner of the pub, is like the majority of wheeries, including his cousin Saffaw, our beloved mall manager. Ready to make a deal with anyone. That is what I concluded when it came to Hammfrual's involvement with the crew of the *Hawk*."

"He and Saffaw are just doing what comes naturally to wheeries." Grannison asked, "Are you, Robert, saying that they have no involvement, whatsoever, in the sabotage? Wasn't Hammfrual the least bit suspicious when the crewmen from the *Hawk* brought Ambassador Calluran into his pub and the ambassador never left?"

Robert answered, "It seems that one of the two crewmen distracted Hammfrual by proposing a deal to purchase several cases of spirits to be transported to their ship. Hammfrual saw nothing but piles of 'stromtha,' the Raushdonian currency, after that. He didn't see the ambassador enter the pub and, since we have kept that fact a secret, neither he nor Saffaw had any reason to suspect anything."

Keanyn was the next to speak. "With that being said, how are we going to move forward in finding out the identity of those two crewmen from the *Hawk*. Where they are now or where they went—assuming they were able to get off this ship before we went into lockdown—and that would almost necessitate finding the location of the *Hawk* itself?"

"I agree," said Stenn. "But, I think I will concentrate on locating the ambassador and how he has eluded detection from our scanners and human searchers. As previously noted, there is some kind of masking technology going on here that is so advanced or that we have never encountered before." He paused before adding, "If it is all right with our captain, and the rest of you, I would like to have Commander Loche assist me since it was his men who discovered where Ambassador Calluran was last seen and the two crewmen who accompanied him."

"While I would be glad to assist you in that, may I suggest using Edward? He needs to get his feet wet in this investigation. And, as he has already demonstrated, his mind is quite adept at picking up clues and properly interpreting them," said Grannison. He added, "I will be happy to supply you with any other assistance as well."

Stenn replied, "I think that will work well, commander." After saying this, Stenn folded his arms and sat back in his chair.

Keanyn now assigned the rest of them to various duties. He began with Mac and Cheng. "I'd like the two of you to continue to try and find clues that will help us decipher this new masking technology that keeps on hindering our investigation. Since a lot of it involves the shuttles and shuttle deck, Cheng has the most knowledge of that area and Mac's science background can help with whatever technologies you uncover that may be too difficult for Cheng to grasp." He held up a hand to stop Cheng's anticipated protest and said, "I am, by no means, questioning your intelligence, Cheng, but Mac is our science officer and has also shown her ability to figure out new and even alien science. Her help in this aspect of our investigation is beyond the abilities of any of the rest of us."

Cheng lowered her head and said, "I see. I promise to help get to the bottom of this masking situation."

"I'm certain that our teamwork will produce results and I will need your skill set to help us reach a satisfactory result," said Mac as she leaned toward Cheng and the two gave each other a fist pump.

"Very good," said Keanyn. "Now, let's move on to Grannison. Commander, I think you will have time to assist Mac and Cheng with your knowledge of masking technology and its specific relationship to onboard ship systems. As I remember, you've already been able to determine a few things."

Grannison responded, "Yes, captain, but most of what I was able to determine is that the terrorists weren't using the standard operation of masking technology. I couldn't figure out the technology behind the form of masking they were employing."

Keanyn spoke with an air of positive hope. "That's true, Grannison, but with the added input of our science officer and keenly observant shuttle deck commander, I'm confident you will be able to discover enough information to help us form a solid idea of how it's being done in order to monitor future attempts to send more enemy operatives onto this vessel. But saying that, we need to have another talk with Salfrod and see if his memory has become any clearer on how his transfer to this ship was accomplished."

Grannison agreed with Keanyn and added, "I believe he may be the key to busting this investigation wide open if he can just get enough of his memory back."

"That's what I hope Robert, ND, and myself will be able to coax out of him, Grann," stated Captain Keanyn Mathews. He then looked around, contemplatively, at everyone and continued. "I've noticed that we have spoken to each other far too formally based on our rank or position on this vessel. I contend that we start to address each other as equals within the confines of our investigative endeavors. Meaning, let's just use our first names. After all, we are all friends and are operating as a group of friends during these investigations. Of course, we will continue to follow proper procedure when we carry out our regular duties."

As he finished this statement all of the others nodded and smiled as they became more relaxed.

Robert added his thoughts. "It is highly unusual to speak to each other so familiarly and I'm wondering how awkward it will feel. Also, there's the chance that we'll slip up and forget when we are going about our regular duties. I admit I was thinking along the same lines as you, captain, but I had to voice my reservations as well."

"That's perfectly fine, Commander Porter—I mean Robert," noted Keanyn. "Yes, we will have to be careful when we're not in our investigative mode, but a slip up here and there shouldn't arouse suspicion."

The others nodded affirmation and the decision was made.

"Also, when talking with Salfrod," Stenn said, returning to the conversation of their stowaway, "If we could present him with the information Grannison has already accumulated, perhaps that will nudge his memory enough to provide us with the further information we need to make a quantum leap toward solving this conundrum."

ND spoke with a gleam in her eyes, "I am in full harmony with that thought, Rob," playfully injecting the new "informal" address into the conversation.

Stenn remarked with a mischievous grin. "Keanyn, I do believe that—as the Brits say—my mum is taking the mickey with you." Looking at ND he said, "I mean, Rob? Really, Mother!"

Keanyn looked completely bewildered by Stenn's comments until ND explained that "take the mickey" was an English expression for poking fun at someone else's expense. As the joke dawned on him, the rest of the room's occupants couldn't hold it in any longer and roared in laughter.

"Okay," Keanyn said. "I guess I had that coming, but you all must agree, being more at ease with each other should help us not feel so pressured to always come up with some breakthrough clue. We don't have to feel like it rests solely on anyone's shoulders to come up with the ultimate solution."

"I don't know about my skills as a detective, Keanyn," said Edward, "but I do have a thought about how we might be able to jog Salfrod's memory as to who lowered the boom on him in the shuttle."

"What's your idea?" asked Robert.

"It occurred to me," began Edward, "that the saying 'a picture is worth a thousand words' might work in Salfrod's case. If we could take him back inside the shuttle, place him where he was before he got hit, and ask him to draw or sketch whatever comes to his mind, it may unlock something trapped in his subconscious."

ND made the next comment. "I've heard of this technique. I believe it's known as 'Visual Memory Stimulation' and has been found to be fairly effective when other methods have failed."

"That's right!" exclaimed Stenn. "We've actually used a form of that when questioning individuals about what they may have witnessed at a crime scene."

Robert said, "As I recall, Stenn, it proved to be very effective in situations where we suspected the witnesses knew more than they were telling us but they didn't know they knew it because it was embedded in their subconscious."

"That is correct, Robert," Concluded ND. "When we encouraged them to try and visualize the scene and then draw or write out what they were seeing, they frequently included details they had forgotten. These details often led to clues that helped us either move ahead or solve a case."

Keanyn stood up to get everyone's attention. He stated, "Edward's suggestion appears to be an excellent one and I've decided that he will accompany ND and myself on our attempt to see if we can bring some more details out of Salfrod's memory that will help us move more decisively forward in solving this most frustrating and sad case. Of course, Grannison will still give you support from time to time. As for Robert, I believe you and our energetic chief engineer have struck up a close friendship. What would you think of enlisting his aid by tapping his knowledge of MLS nine, Multi-Light Speed, and masking techniques with the excuse that you just want to pick his brain?"

"That's an interesting coincidence, Keanyn," said Robert. "Because we have often engaged in picking each other's brains in just that manner. So he should not be suspicious that I am trying to get information from him for another reason."

"Very good!" exclaimed Keanyn. "Additionally, I would like you to give whatever info you get to Mac and between the three of you, we might get a handle on this masking technique. Of course, Mac and Cheng are going to be working on the shuttles. I would hope that with all that effort, we will be able to come up with a solution to this dilemma."

With everyone now assigned, Keanyn dismissed the meeting, wishing everyone good success, and, as they filed out, Stenn leaned forward to whisper into Robert's ear, "Realistically, what do you think of our chances?"

Robert looked as if he were figuring up the odds and responded, "I wouldn't have given us much hope at all a week or two ago. But now I think we've got some solid ideas on how to pry loose some of those vital memories from Salfrod's brain. I feel much like Grannison when he said he felt the key to arriving at the solution to who the accomplice on board this ship is our congenial stowaway."

Stenn replied, "Revealing that identity could also lead to unraveling a lot more concerning the sabotage plot. If we can couple jogging Salfrod's memory with solving the masking technology, we could probably begin to clear up this entire investigation."

Mac and Cheng joined them on their way to the shuttle bay. Robert would use the shuttle bay entrance to the engineering deck to talk to Chief Stokely. The shuttle bay entrance was not used nearly as much as the main entrance located just between the anteroom entrance to the mall and the large vestibule that served as an introductory area showcasing all the amazing aspects of the grandiose shopping and entertainment venue that was the main feature of the starship *Cosmic Mall.*

Suddenly, alarms went off and Robert immediately checked his comm device to find out what was going on.

"What's the matter?" questioned Mac excitedly.

Robert said, "My chief security officer in the mall, Ross Carter, says someone drove one of the alien transports they sell there into the center court and ran it into the protective view wall that surrounds the waterfall and breached it, causing a significant leak that's beginning to flood the center courts first level."

His answer made them think, *Oh No! What else can go wrong!*

Cheng asked. "Do you need us to go with you?"

"No," returned Robert. "This may just be an accident. One of the customers may have gotten overexuberant as they were test-driving the transport and lost control. If it is something more sinister, I'll be sure to inform you. On second thought, I think I'll ask Stenn to go with me. Cheng, you and Mac need to get started breaking down the other transporting problem we have."

Mac turned to look at Cheng saying, "Let's hope they don't discover that it's any more than an accident. I think we're getting down to the nitty-gritty of this investigation, with what we may or may not find out during these next endeavors."

"I couldn't agree with you more, Mac," stated Cheng. "Robert and Stenn will be very thorough, I'm sure, and if it is anything more than an accident, they will get to the bottom of it."

CHAPTER TWO

AN ACCIDENT OR MORE SABOTAGE?

When Robert and Stenn arrived at the mall's center court there was pandemonium. Water was steadily streaming from the waterfall but was kept from spreading into the main concourse by Ross Carter's quick thinking. He had raced to the closest custodial station and, with the help of someone from security and three from the custodial staff, got every dry vac machine and a large turbo fan keeping the water from exiting the center court into the concourse and several of the stores nearby.

The dry vacs were extra large industrial-strength machines that could scoop up more than seven times the quantity of water than the regular commercial ones. They also contained super large reservoirs with extra powerful evaporating devices. They were using three of them and barely staying ahead of the flow.

The turbo fan was used to serve as a powerful wind machine that made the water flow backward in a wave pattern of about one to two feet in height. Needless to say, the rest of the security and custodial staff made certain all of the customers and restaurant/shop workers were ushered out of harm's way.

"How long do you think you can keep the water from going into the main concourse?" Robert asked Ross.

"Not much longer!" Ross yelled. "We've got to get that breach closed in the waterfall casing."

Robert shouted at Stenn due to the volume of sound coming from the exposed waterfall, "Stenn, can you see what can be done to close the breach?"

"I'm three steps ahead of you, Robert," answered Ross. "I've called the botanists to give us a hand. They will be here in a few seconds."

"The botanists!" screamed Robert in disbelief. "What in the galaxy could they do to help us?"

"They aren't merely plant and flower people. They do maintenance on all of the displays that feature plants and flowers. The waterfall, while spectacular, is a grand flower display," Ross explained.

At that moment, Stella Steel and Laurindo kwark arrived with several others from botany, entered the breach in the view wall, and began erecting a secondary section in the wall. This kept the flooding waters contained within the waterfall display. The only downside was that the leaking waters were now flooding a much smaller area that was filling up quickly, threatening to drown the workers inside.

"They'd better be quick," noted Stenn. "That chamber

will fill up in no time. Is there some way we can help them or create an escape for them?"

Ross Carter spoke with confidence, "I think you'll find that they have already fixed the most immediate problem of keeping the water from flooding or damaging any more of the mall."

As they watched, the waters of the cascade began to slow and then shrink to a trickle. The startled onlookers first looked at the scene of the dried-up waterfall then at Ross, who explained, "That crew of botanists and their helpers are equipped with a special tool that is used to turn the falls on and off. As soon as they got inside the containment area, one of them dove into the pool and swam to a control arm at the base of the falls. They then used that tool to slowly turn the flow of water off. You have to be an exceptional swimmer able to hold your breath for quite a while to do this."

"Why not use a wet suit and breathing device?" queried Robert.

"Because the small chamber is very, very tight and a breathing device wouldn't allow a person to effectively use the tool," explained Ross.

"Sounds like a terrible design flaw to me," noted Stenn.

Ross stated, "Oh, that it is, but the botany crew takes some sort of weird pride in being able to accomplish it."

Robert then directed everyone to an important observation. "Where is the driver that caused this catastrophe?"

The rest stopped in their tracks as the implications of that statement hit them.

Ross voiced another startling question, "Where did Stenn get to? He was here just a minute ago!"

"If I know Stenn, and I do, he's off tracking down the perpetrator of this incident," declared Robert.

And that was indeed where he was!

Stenn had noticed the vehicle that caused the breach in the waterfall's protective wall had been moved but no one was either inside it or being held by security anywhere nearby. When he questioned Ross's staff, they said there was no one in or near the vehicle when they arrived.

"Then that makes it a hit and run!" exclaimed Stenn. "Didn't you think to ask someone what they might have seen so that you could get a lead on tracking down this character?" He was disappointed in the lack of efficiency demonstrated by a staff trained by Ross Carter.

The head officer, Tad Stovall, blushed deeply and said, "We're sorry, sir. We got so busy with helping escort people out of harm's way that we failed to give thought to the cause of the accident."

Stenn quickly started asking as many as he could if they had seen anything and someone told him she had seen two humans emerge from the vehicle and just blend into the crowd. He obtained a reasonably good description of two men dressed in maintenance uniforms, wearing tool belts, who briskly walked away from the scene.

Stenn began to run swiftly in the direction the two men had taken. This happened to be directly toward the Frothy Mug pub. When he arrived there, he found Hammfrual, the proprietor, and Saffaw, his cousin, sitting at a table drinking leisurely.

"I hope you two aren't involved in the vandalism at the waterfall!" he stated rather angrily. Their response stopped him short.

Saffaw said, "You mean the two maintenance men we're holding in the latrine that's typically used for those who've become violently sick from overindulgence?" They both had broad smiles on their faces.

"What!" yelled Stenn incredulously. He calmed down and continued. "Well, at least, I see you had the good sense to detain them in the proper location. I can't even think of a description for the odors spewing from that latrine. I'm sure they will regret their actions after spending time in that torture chamber."

The two Raushdonians explained that they had noticed the furtive movements of the maintenance workers and decided to position themselves where they could catch their conversation. After listening to just a few minutes of their discussion, they surmised that they had something to do with the crash at the waterfall and decided to corral them in the latrine.

They escorted Stenn to the latrine and all three held their noses as the door was unlocked and opened. To say that what wafted out of that chamber was potent was like saying that rotten eggs coupled with human excrement was a pleasant perfume.

Stenn immediately gagged and began to vomit. Hammfrual choked on his bile and even Saffaw began popping mints and spraying fresh scent (which had no effect!) in the air.

The two prisoners were out cold from the stench and had to be dragged out into the storage room of the pub, where the atmosphere was much sweeter.

Once revived and tied to chairs, the two maintenance workers stared ahead as if they couldn't figure out where they were. As their minds slowly cleared of the miasma from their prison, they noticed the individuals standing before them. Captain Mathews, security chiefs Robert Porter and Ross Carter, Stenn, and the mall manager Saffaw formed a semi-circle around them—and they did not look happy to see them.

Stenn had called the others informing them that they were holding the two they believed were responsible for the vandalism at the center court's first level. They had arrived barely a minute before the vandals had become lucid.

Robert Porter was the first to speak. "We are currently checking to verify whether you are actually maintenance employees of the mall, but Saffaw here says he has seen you working on the custodial staff before so you are probably legit. What we want to know is"—he looked at them with his cold ominous stare—"what was your reason for crashing into the waterfall display? Was it a genuine accident or a premeditated act of violence?" Robert lowered his voice, pitching it deep to create a sense of danger. "If you are part of whatever was behind the A deck catastrophe be assured, our judgment will be swift and very unpleasant!"

Captain Mathews quickly interjected, "But not until we have thoroughly wrung every bit of information out of you."

The miscreants stared defiantly back at the captain and one of them spoke with a sneer on his face. "Do what you can to us, Mathews. Just let it be known that we were proud to cause you and your pathetic *Mall* any damage we could."

His partner, encouraged by his comrade's statement, added, "That's right! We only wish we could have carried out more destruction. Your miserable contribution to the Galactic Legion will prove to be a complete failure as the more astute member planets realize it's a total waste of time and money!"

Stenn stepped forward and back-handed the second man, Samuel Harris, in the face. Robert quickly intervened and held Stenn back from a second blow saying, "It's not that we all wouldn't like to do the same thing, Stenn, but we need to get information from them and we can't do that if they're beaten unconscious."

Stenn apologized and said, "It's just all of the stress of the last several days caught up with me when I heard the hate in this man's voice."

Keanyn acknowledged Stenn's stress by saying, "We all have been stressed out and the actions of these two slime bags hasn't helped. But we need to find out what the motivation behind their actions is." He turned to the first of the supposed maintenance workers, Charles Saxby, and asked, "Who put you up to this stunt?"

Saxby smirked and answered, "Wouldn't you like to know? I'll bet it would scare you to death if we are just one of many arms of the sabotage plot against this ship and its mission."

At that moment, Robert's private comm line blinked and he took a message from ND. He smiled as he turned to Saxby and Harris and said, "It's really funny when a lone wolf tries to act like he's a full-fledged member of the pack. You guys talk a big game, but you're just a couple of small-time thugs."

Harris countered with, "You're bluffing. You have no way of knowing if we're part of the conspiracy or just a couple of loose cannons!"

"As a matter of fact, I have it on good authority that you two are a couple of disgruntled rebels against the Legion that never wanted to see the Earth join. You were arrested some twelve years ago and were released seven years later and applied for positions as maintenance workers on the *Mall* starship because you wanted to cause mischief as you were against the project. No one has contacted you about joining a sabotage plot because they didn't even know you existed," proclaimed Robert.

"How do you know all of that?" Saxby said, effectively admitting to the security chief that his claims were legitimate.

"Keep your trap shut you idiot!" shouted Harris.

With no further reason to question the two concerning their involvement in a plot, the group of interrogators went back to their responsibilities, leaving Stenn and Robert to retrieve any loose ends and put the two vandals in the brig awaiting a trial in the Earth embassy on Janos.

Later, Keanyn stopped Robert as he was exiting the mall after making sure the repairs to the waterfall dome were being made. Keanyn asked him anxiously, "How long will it be before the center court and the surrounding area are back to normal?"

"The damage was surprisingly less than it appeared at first, and with the equipment that Stella Steel and Larindo kwark have at their disposal, a few days should suffice. Plus, there is a lot of manpower from maintenance. They consider it their duty to clean up the damage two of their own created." Robert paused, then continued, "You wouldn't have waited around here for me to get done just to ask about repairs. You want to know how I knew to call the bluff of those troublemakers?"

Keanyn nodded his head and said, "I suspected the comm you received shortly before your exposure of the maintenance duo contained the information you made known."

"That, and some facts I already knew, made the amateur attempt at sabotage by Harris and Saxby clear. ND informed me that our two miscreants had served time as rebels, and could not have been recruited by our main saboteurs as they seem to have been organized while these two were serving their sentences and no one recruited anyone from Earth's prisons to join their conspiracy. When they became employees of the *Mall* starship, there was no record of anyone contacting them. That's the bit of information I had. So they weren't much of a threat to begin with." He looked at Keanyn with relief.

Keanyn smiled, shook his head, and addressed Robert, saying, "While it is a relief that those two were operating independently, it does indicate that we need to be diligent about further incidents."

"I'm already formulating plans along those lines. Among other things, I'm going to use Ross Carter more extensively," noted Robert thoughtfully.

CHAPTER THREE

STENN'S SPECIAL ASSIGNMENT

Mac and Cheng were busy studying the vid records from the shuttle that Salfrod had been discovered on as an injured stowaway. This must have been the tenth time they had done so but they knew they must be missing something vitally important. As they closely watched the vid, they were startled when Robert and Stenn came into the room with no announcement.

"Doesn't anyone from security have any idea what proper etiquette is?" questioned Cheng.

Stenn answered, "I would have thought we were expected. You do want a report on that incident in the mall, don't you?" His lips curled up in a mischievous smile and Robert outwardly chuckled.

It was Mac who spoke next, saying, "You could easily have told us of the mall situation via your comm unit. I believe you just wanted to make yourselves look important by way of a face-to-face report. Besides, we already know the outcome."

"I think you should appreciate the fact we took the time to personally come here and inform you. After all, we all have other important responsibilities to handle," noted Robert in a mocked hurtful voice.

"Just as you said, Robert. We all have important tasks. That is all but one of us! Stenn, I don't believe I heard Keanyn assign you any particular task. Other than the one you assigned to yourself," Mac said, as she focused her curiously amusing stare on the ship's covert investigative operative.

Stenn smiled slily and answered Mac in his usual evasive manner. "Why, you must not have been paying attention when the captain gave me my assignment, Mac."

"Come to think of it, I must have been similarly distracted," stated Cheng, as she began to peer suspiciously at Stenn. "He never did give you the 'okay' to go ahead with your idea."

Robert leaned casually against the bulkhead of the room with a grin on his face and said, "I think they've got you to rights on this one, my friend, because I don't recall hearing Keanyn give you an assignment either. Of course, I'm used to you having duties to perform that are known only to yourself, but since we were all in the room together and received assignments, the absence of one for you was rather glaring and, no doubt, stirred up the curiosity of these two observant officers and ladies."

"Well, if I can't rely on help from my trusted friend and confidant, I guess I must take these two fine 'officers and ladies,' as you so tactfully put it, into my confidence as well." Stenn shrugged his shoulders in acquiescence. "Keanyn spoke to me a few minutes before our meeting and asked if I would mind going down to the surface of Janos and look into a bit of information he had received from the defense minister of the planet. It had to deal with a seemingly insignificant detail concerning an unauthorized shipment of parts for the guidance systems of their mining probe machines. As it was a fairly benign piece of equipment and they had already received a shipment recently, they just chalked it up to an error of duplication, which happens from time to time. The only thing that made this incident curious was that the order was not sent to the main mining warehouse but was sent to a private residence."

"I imagine that the private residence rang some alarm bells in Keanyn's mind?" Robert guessed.

"Spoken like a true chief of security," noted Stenn. "Yes, that private residence was the home of the ambassador to Janos from, guess where?"

"Saffo V!" declared Cheng as if she had discovered the location of a long-lost treasure.

"Exactly!" answered Stenn. "Yes, the home of our beloved Ambassador Calluran. And, though that fact would not have raised the suspicions of the Janovian Defense Minister, it raised an entire fleet of red flags as far as Keanyn was concerned."

Mac questioned Stenn, "Why did the minister bring up the incident to the captain in the first place?"

"It was similar to what they were already discussing," said Stenn, then added, "Keanyn had been explaining to the minister how products purchased at the mall remotely were shipped and what a logistics nightmare it could be having to ship them all over the Legion's interplanetary territory. The minister then brought up the fact that they had experienced delivery glitches on occasion themselves, citing the example of the mining parts."

"That's one coincidence I am grateful for," stated Robert. "And you know how I feel about coincidence. A real coincidence rarely happens, but this may be one of them."

Cheng made a remark that caused both Stenn and Robert to take notice. She said, "This particular coincidence has all the markings of what my grandfather would have called providential. And, if that's the case it makes it a premeditated incident, which would take it out of the realm of coincidence."

Robert and Stenn looked at each other, blinked, and shook their heads vigorously as if to clear them of that last thought. Mac noticed their actions and said, "What's wrong, you two? You're acting as though you don't believe in providence. Granted, as a person of science, I've had difficulty in believing in something or someone controlling the universe and I never would have thought that that entity would concern itself with an individual, but I've read about, experienced, and researched enough incidents to seriously consider the possibility."

Robert chose to speak for both himself and Stenn by responding to Mac's comment. "Stenn, his mother, and I have had a few discussions on this subject and I will say that while we may not be 'believers' we are neither 'doubters' on this subject. Suffice it to say that the jury is still out where we're concerned. We're not fence sitters just still researching."

"But as to this particular incident of the discussion between the captain and the Janovian minister, I tend to lead toward coincidence," said Stenn.

"With that cleared up," Cheng said sarcastically, "just

what do you think about the possible ramifications of this mistakenly shipped order going to the home of the Saffo V Ambassador to Janos?"

"I don't want to presume anything until I get down there and see what I can find out," stated Stenn. "But I am glad that you questioned me on what my assignment was because I can now accompany you and Mac to the shuttle deck and not have to try and get passage to the planet on a shuttle and invent a reason for going or get around answering a lot of questions. Even though that is part of my job description, it's nice to get a break from all of the subterfuge." As he said this, Stenn appeared to visibly relax and was almost casual in his demeanor, something rarely seen in him.

Robert opined, "If I were to speculate, I would guess that this has something to do with Ambassador Calluran's involvement in the sabotage and his whereabouts since. He disappeared right at the exact time of the A deck tragedy and he hasn't been found anywhere on the ship."

Mac spoke next, "Are you thinking he was transported down to the planet using that unknown masking technology?"

"It wouldn't be a long shot if he was," said Robert. "But, as Stenn said, we don't want to form conclusions that could crowd out recognizing any other scenario. After all, there might be nothing to this at all but the innocent mistake of the shipper."

"Yeah, and I believe that Sharlees have never played practical jokes on anyone," scoffed Cheng.

"We've hung around here a little too long. We need to go to work," Stenn declared.

"I agree," said Robert. "Our chief engineer is a pretty sharp fellow when it comes to figuring things out. If he sees through my inquiries then I may have to ask if we can add another person to our team."

"Frankly, I think that might be a good thing," noted Stenn.

CHAPTER FOUR

THE LEGION ARRIVES

Captain Keanyn Mathews was in the command chair on the bridge of the starship *Cosmic Mall* mulling over all the information the investigative team had discovered concerning the recent sabotage and what he, ND, and Edward had just found out in their latest interview with Salfrod.

The possibility he had suggested by his memory jog had been almost inconceivable. Keanyn's meditations were interrupted by J. A. Philpot, the ship's communication officer, who had just received a communication from Legion headquarters.

"I'm sorry to disturb your meditations, captain, but I thought you would like to know that the Legion investigative division's team will be arriving at 0800 hours tomorrow and they have requested a full briefing meeting at 0830. Commander Dek from the internal affairs division will be heading up the Legion's investigation into our 'recent problem,' as they have termed it." JA grimaced, indicating his distaste at having to deliver the message.

Keanyn responded, "Well, they're sending 'Dek the Dupe' to get to the bottom of our little incident." He had a pronounced smirk on his face.

"But why internal affairs?" asked Mac from her chair at the science station. "Shouldn't it be from the investigative and detection division?"

Not for the first time, Keanyn looked at Mac, noticing the flow of her stunning auburn hair as it rolled down her shoulders. He also took note, for the hundredth time, of the shape of her face, the fullness of her lips, and the emerald sparkle of her eyes.

Before anyone could wonder at his pause in responding to Mac's questions, he brought himself out of his mental assessments and stated, "I assume, Lieutenant Stinson, that certain factions within the Legion's command staff would love to rub our faces in it by suggesting that the sabotage and subsequent loss of so many lives was due to, either, ineptitude within our own investigations prior to the incident or collusion with the saboteurs by someone within the ship's officers or crew."

"What a monumental insult!" declared Mac as the color in her face became a hot red.

Grannison spoke from his station, in front and to the right just below the platform on which sat the captain's chair. "Some within the command staff not only want to insult us, but their intention is even to disgrace us and derail our mission."

"I would have thought that the success we had obtained up to that point and the overall positive feedback we had received from the planets we had visited would have calmed the most vehement feelings that had been voiced or acted upon before our mission began," stated Carl Burdgess, who was currently manning the navigational station. His six-foot-two muscular frame and dark brown hair was in sharp contrast to his assistant navigator Edward's lean frame and blond hair.

Grannison brought Carl up to speed on the discontent that many still felt toward the *Cosmic Mall* project. "It's impossible to change someone's mind on something they have strong feelings about, Lieutenant Burdgess," he said. "Especially when those feelings include hatred. And, don't kid yourself, son, the poison that hatred can contribute to almost any situation is extremely volatile. When this ship was launched with the blessing of most in the Legion's command and then proved so well received by the first four ports of call, it just angered those who still harbored hatred for the Earth and its contribution to the Legion. They were just waiting for an opportunity to pounce and they've taken advantage of it." Grannison leaned forward in his chair with a look on his face of sternness and a little wrath. Everyone on the bridge was glad that look was not directed toward them.

"You speak for me as well, commander," added Keanyn. "I would also like to know why Commander Dek was chosen. His reputation as a puppet controlled by others worries me."

Mac joined in the conversation again. "If you're worried that Commander Dek will have an agenda beyond merely investigating the sabotage then may I suggest something from the female point of view?"

"You pique my curiosity, Miss Stinson," said Keanyn. "Go right ahead and we'll see if the feminine touch is what we need."

"First of all, captain," said Mac. "You said the commander is controlled by others so why can't we try to control him to some degree from this end?"

"I like where I think you're going, lieutenant commander," said Grannison. "If I've guessed right, do you plan on doing this yourself?"

Mac responded, "No, commander. But I do have someone specific in mind."

"Now wait just one minute, you two!" broke in the captain with frustration. "Commander Loche may have guessed where you're going with this, but I'm completely in the dark. What do you mean by controlling Commander Dek from this end?"

"What I mean, captain," said Mac, "is assigning an attentive female companion to Commander Dek while he is here could serve as enough of a distraction to take his mind off some of the additional investigations he may be doing for others. It has to be someone who is fairly attractive but able to derive helpful information from him without arousing his suspicions."

The captain then asked her, "That all sounds good but who's the young lady you have in mind?"

"I think I could venture a guess," stated Grannison. "Would Lindsey Thompson be your choice?"

"Spot on, commander!" answered Mac in an excited tone. "Not only is Lindsey easy to look at, but she has brains to go along with the looks. Also, in one of our conversations, she told me how she had used her physical beauty to flatter men into giving her some trinkets or information she had desired. We're not talking sensitive information or even minor trade secrets but the principle is the same."

Keanyn had a look of concern as he said, "I don't know if I want to put a member of our crew in the kind of potential danger this scenario suggests."

Mac understood Keanyn's concern as she said, "I appreciate that, as captain, you feel a strong sense of responsibility toward all the members of this crew. As you should, I might add, sir. Therefore, what if I promise to speak to Lieutenant Thompson and feel her out about this? I will make certain she understands the risk, but, also, the importance of this endeavor."

Keanyn spoke cautiously, saying, "You have my permission to speak to our tech officer, lieutenant, but any—and I repeat ANY—reluctance on Miss Thompson's part will scrap this idea."

"Aye, aye, sir!" was Mac's emphatic reply.

It was an unusual occurrence for the members of the investigative team to discuss their intended activities on the bridge in front of Carl Burdgess and JA, who were not privy to their endeavors. Keanyn realized that they had let their guard down, but hoped that Carl and JA would just take their comments as merely general conversation and concern for the Legion's investigation causing problems for the ship's officers and crew. To lessen any chance that they might suspect something, he casually asked them, "Do you and Ensign Philpot have any thoughts as to this Legion investigation, Lieutenant Burdgess? Since we're on shutdown, we are only complying with our shift schedules by being on the bridge in the first place. All we have to do, for the time being, is monitor the ship's systems so it's a good time to get everyone's thoughts on our predicament."

They were both considering Keanyn's question concerning the Legion's intrusion when Carl spoke up. "It's not that we weren't expecting their arrival, but I'm not happy that they're taking it from the internal affairs division. That demonstrates a lack of trust in us that I don't see as justified."

JA added his thoughts. "That's right, sir. Where, in all

the mess surrounding the sabotage, was there even a hint of collusion on the part of anyone on board this ship?"

Carl spoke in a tone that suggested he had realized something. "There is the stowaway. I've heard that he may have had help from someone on board and that someone was the one who knocked him unconscious. That seems to me to be a possibility for internal affairs."

"Maybe so," said JA. "But I can't believe that it could be anyone from the military contingent. There are plenty from the mall staff that it might be. Not that I suspect anyone in particular, it's just that they're not trained to defend this ship and its mission as we are. Their responsibilities lie with the success of their retail goals."

Keanyn took up the conversation again, saying, "I'm very glad you two voiced your thoughts. They've given me something to think about concerning the Legion's duties when they arrive on the ship. Although, I'm not exactly sure what I can do about it, apart from the suggestion of Lieutenant Commander Stinson."

Keanyn purposely dumbed down his comment to keep Carl and JA from suspecting that there was a lot Keanyn and his team could and would do to make certain they were not kept in the dark when the Legion began trying to unravel the murderous plot of the saboteurs. In fact, some of the things JA and Carl said made him realize an important aspect of their investigations that had been either overlooked or brushed aside. The *Mall* personnel.

He wondered if he could trust Suffaw enough to see if he could do a little digging for them concerning the mall staff. Suffaw was a real wheeler-dealer as well as the manager of the mall and, as such, knew a lot about the people who worked there. That would also include knowing things about them they may not have wanted known. He could be a real source of information to them, but at what cost? And with Suffaw there was always a price.

Well, thought Keanyn to himself, *I'll just have to broach the subject to the team and see how it flies — though it will probably crash*. He smiled ruefully at the possibility of the idea's success.

After her shift on the bridge, Mac went back to the shuttle bay to join Cheng in the continuance of their labors into the advanced masking technologies used by the "Sabotage Conspiracy," as they were now calling it. When she arrived at the deck, she immediately found the lieutenant in the control hub, the center that correlated all of the arrivals and departures from the ship. Cheng was glued to a view screen, pouring over data.

"You'll go blind doing that, lieutenant," said Mac as she approached Cheng.

Cheng raised up, jerking her head back to throw her long black hair behind her back, and retorted with, "I seem to recall you in the same position seconds before you left for your shift on the bridge, ma'am. I don't think there's anything wrong with your eyesight and you probably look at view screens twice as much as I do."

"That's true, but I've developed a system wherein I am able to save my eyes from becoming fatigued," stated Mac with an air of supremacy.

Cheng countered with, "I don't think it's working because you obviously missed seeing the sign on the door to this control center that says 'DO NOT ENTER; AUTHORIZED PERSONNEL ONLY' in all caps and twice the size of any other signs in the shuttle bay."

"Since I *am* an authorized person, maybe it's your

memory that's not working instead of your eyes," returned Mac.

Cheng couldn't keep a snort of laughter from escaping her mouth.

Once they gained their composure, Mac asked Cheng, "Have you been able to isolate the contents of that wispy puff of smoke that appeared just milliseconds before Salfrod appeared in the shuttle?"

"It seems to contain a very small amount of the chemical kherzodine which can only be found in the Sagittarius Dwarf Elliptical Galaxy. Or more precisely, when that elliptical galaxy passed through the core of the Milky Way causing perturbations in some of the stars there and forming new or altered chemicals such as kherzodine."

Mac was truly astounded at the depth of Cheng's astronomical intelligence and said, "My goodness, Cheng! I had no idea that your galactic know-how was as complete as that! You are matchless when it comes to logistics and getting the most and best out of people, but I didn't know you possessed such skills when it came to the workings of the galaxy."

"Before you start awarding me doctorates in chemistry and astronomy, I must tell the truth," said Cheng. "When it comes to my knowledge of the galaxy and its inner workings, I dropped out of school, remember? But I am a good reader and you were gone long enough that I looked up kherzodine on the ship's computer and read all that info. I memorized it so I could repeat it to you as if I knew it. And, by the way, that certainly proves that there is nothing wrong with my memory!" She said this last statement with a defiant look and her hands on her hips.

"Bravo and touchè!" exclaimed Mac. "I respect that. You recognize your limitations and make up for them through hard work and initiative. That's better than one hundred doctorates."

Cheng was now blushing three shades of red and sheepishly said, "I didn't know where I was headed when my family was captured and arrested. I knew it wasn't going to be good. But then I was given this second chance and my lovely grandmother, who had never given up hope for me, told me not to squander this opportunity, I knew I had to make it work. If what you just said is even half true then I have made my grandmother proud."

Mac said, "I'm sure you have. That is an important discovery you made. I can make some links that will help us resolve this problem. But we'll need some input from Robert first."

"That's right," said Cheng. "We are supposed to team up with him and see if his discussions with Chief Stokes have shed any light on how our enemies are able to transport people on and off this ship without our notice. How often has engineering teamed up with physics, and now apparently chemistry, to solve issues?"

Mac answered, "More times than you might think. The various sciences, though possessing different aspects and applications, have been shown to have an amazing ability to work with one another, no matter how much the various scientists claim that their particular branch is superior to others."

"That sounds a bit petty of ones we think of as highly intelligent," said Cheng with a look of bewilderment on her face.

"Believe me, Cheng, no one has cornered the market on pettiness. There's plenty left to go around and scientists have collected their fair share of it," stated Mac.

"By the way, commander, Robert said it would be relatively easy to bring up this subject with Stokes as they had frequently engaged in such mental exercises before so it wouldn't arouse his suspicions," remarked Cheng.

Mac responded, "If Robert presented it to him as a result of talking to you about the situation you have been dealing with concerning the stowaway and how he was transported to one of your shuttles undetected, it would pass without arousing Stokes's suspicions."

"Okay," said Cheng. "I'll give Robert a call and see if he can join us."

On the next morning, at precisely 0800 hours on the shuttle deck, the investigative contingent from the Legion arrived. They were welcomed by Captain Keanyn Mathews, science officer Lieutenant Commander MacCardle Stinson, Chief Stokely Davis, Doctor Alfred Karushkin, and, of course, the shuttle bay commander, Lieutenant Cheng Wong.

The absence of the ship's liaison ambassador Yahnsoof Calluran was immediately addressed by the head investigator of the group, Commander Raxton Dek, a Plumator from the planet Nanior, the fourth planet in the Pictor constellation. Plumators are humanoids who possess what appears to be scaly armor from their chests down to the lower abdomen and a short tail-like protrusion from their lower spine. They proudly display their armored chests by wearing clothing that is always open in that area. Their 'tails' are exposed as well and are of various colors, ranging from a dull green to a vibrant orange. The vibrancy of those colors is enhanced artificially as a sign of the Plumator's rank (if military) or station (political or social). Commander Dek's 'tail' was a bright blue denoting his high (but not highest) ranking in the military.

He addressed the welcoming committee from the starship just after the initial greetings. "I would have expected the presence of your distinguished liaison officer, Ambassador Calluran," Dek said with annoyance. "I met the ambassador years ago and was captivated by his knowledge and wit. I was so looking forward to meeting him again. Is there something wrong with his health?"

He made this inquiry as if to say, "That would be the only reason I could imagine that would prevent him from being here to meet *me*!"

Keanyn, seething inside but keeping his composure, said, "My apologies, Commander Dek, but our esteemed ambassador has gone missing." After gasps and other shocked expressions, the captain continued with his explanation. "It occurred simultaneously with the tragic incident on the A deck and may very well have had something to do with it. There are very few clues to give us any idea as to its significance in that regard. In fact, I can't even tell you if the ambassador's disappearance was an abduction or voluntary."

"While I can't begin to imagine that he would disappear of his own accord at such a critical time," stated Commander Dek with an air of audacity, "my question to you, captain, is why didn't we know about this in the first place?"

Keanyn was a little embarrassed that they had kept the ambassador's disappearance away from the Legion, but, without any concrete evidence one way or another as to his duplicity in the sabotage plot or any real clues that he hadn't vanished on his own, there was little they could tell them other than the fact that he was gone and they didn't know why.

After Keanyn had explained, he motioned the group to follow his welcoming team. It seemed, though, that

Commander Dek still wasn't satisfied with the Captain's explanation and voiced his concerns.

"Your actions concerning this cover-up of the whereabouts of the ambassador seem highly suspicious to me and could result in action being taken against you and your fellow officers when this is reported back to the admiralty."

Robert Porter had joined the group on the shuttle deck as Keanyn was beginning his explanation of Calluran's disappearance and was now as angry as he had ever been.

It took a monumental effort to calm himself down, but he approached Commander Dek as he finished his threat against the captain and his officers and got right up in his face. He spoke in a quiet but threatening voice as he said, "Commander Dek. I am Lieutenant Commander Robert Porter, the head of security on this ship. I have several years of experience in, not only security but, espionage and undercover surveillance. I was the one who advised Captain Mathews to hold off on reporting the disappearance of Ambassador Calluran for, not only the reasons he cited, but, also, important security purposes. So if you want to question the actions of anyone it should be me." Now Robert put his right index finger up immediately in front of Dek's face and said, "But I warn you, sir! If you try to take any action against the command staff of this ship, you will be facing countercharges from me, personally, concerning your incompetence in accusing people before you've even, officially, begun your inquiries. And don't think I can't make those charges stick!"

Commander Dek recoiled in undisguised fear. The rest of his group, which included two military policemen from a class at the same school as Robert, two more detectives that had received training from the internal affairs division's eight-week course, took two steps back as well. The two MPs did so with a look of respect toward Robert. They had heard about this cocky but brilliant alum and now they saw that the stories about him were accurate. The sixth person in the group, who was an "IA" underling serving as eyes for the Legion who passed on orders directly from IA to Commander Dek, was already standing several feet behind the rest and making notations on a "trans-pad," an electro-digital notepad that also served as a digital communications unit. His notations were automatically getting back to someone at Legion HQ.

Commander Dek nervously smoothed his uniform with his hands to buy time in order to get his composure then said, "I will take your statement under advisement, commander. In the meantime, we must move on and get this investigation underway. I believe we have a meeting scheduled for 0830 hours. Where are we to convene that meeting Captain Mathews?"

Keanyn gave a little start as if he hadn't been a participant in the conversation and answered, "I'm sorry, commander, to have spent so much time here. Our meeting is arranged in the council chambers of Mr. Porter's quarters just some fifty yards down the corridor aft of this shuttle bay."

"Very well, captain," said Dek as he and the rest of his party were ushered toward the rear of the bay.

Two hours into the meeting, it had been made clear that the Legion's investigators had an agenda that paid very little attention to the onboard investigation of Keanyn's team or ignored it altogether. They were going to go full steam ahead with their plan, leaning strongly in the direction of digging up as much evidence of incompetency on the command staff as they could. Even to the point of making it up! In order to prove that, the A deck tragedy was either an accident due to said incompetency or a conspiracy from within to sabotage the mission of the starship *Cosmic Mall*.

While the second scenario had some amount of truth to it, the source of the sabotage was not from within the ship but from without, using individuals planted in the ship. Keanyn and his team had vehemently tried to get Dek and his two detectives to see that but there was no moving them from their position.

Dek had just made the insulting statement that one or more of these conspirators were probably in that very room—while looking straight at Robert—when the head of security stood up and said, "Gentlemen, and I use that term loosely"—looking at Dek and his entourage. "If the captain will permit me, I think it is time we adjourned this meeting so that the commander and his team may actually begin their 'investigations,' and the rest of us can get on with our duties, sir." As he said this last word, he turned to Keanyn to get his approval and received a firm nod of his head.

As they filed out of the room, Mac whispered to Keanyn, "I'm glad Robert kept his head and said what he did because I was probably ten seconds away from throwing my comm unit at Dek and calling him a jerk."

Keanyn replied, "I'm glad you didn't, but you would have had to stand in line behind me."

Robert stopped Mac and Cheng in the corridor just after Dek's team entered the anteroom that led onto the A deck. Dek had wanted to begin his investigation there, and while that wasn't a bad choice, Robert would have chosen the A deck control room because that's where the sabotage occurred.

He began by saying, "Were you able to isolate the kherzodine from the other elements in that puff of smoke, Mac?"

"Yes." She said, "I discovered just what Stokes suspected. When it combines with the other elements in the formula that makes up the propulsion, generating the power behind the masking technology, it speeds up the transfer so that it can't be detected by our current sensors."

"When I talked to Stokes," declared the security chief. "He said he knew that something was getting past the detector sensors and he thought that it was a speed issue. When I told him about the kherzodine, he immediately felt that was the answer. He said since he couldn't find a solution via the engineering route, it made sense that it would have to be from another source, and physics and/or chemistry had to be the answer. He said to give the information to you, Mac, because he didn't possess the knowledge of physics that you do." Robert added, "But the next question is are we able to update our systems to detect this new masking technique?"

Mac answered, "After we talked yesterday, I thought we would have to use kherzodine in order to speed up our detection systems and, of course, we don't have any on board. We wouldn't, would we, because it's a relatively new discovery that there were no known uses in any of our current systems."

"Until now," chimed in Cheng.

"Exactly!" said Mac. "So I started looking through my research on 'trilliatide' and remembered that when dealing with newly discovered or alien physics, there was often a known element or combination of elements that either mimicked or replicated the formerly unknown element."

Robert jumped in with, "So I'm guessing you found something."

"Just so," said Mac. "I'm not going to bore you with the

details, but I came up with a formula that will even excel their masking technology."

"How easily can it be implemented?" Cheng asked.

Mac responded, "It will take a little time. We have to dismantle our detecting mechanisms and insert the new propulsion formula which I and a few others can make up in my lab. I'll need help to speed up the process. Then reinstall the updated detectors. All of that shouldn't take more than three or four days."

"In the meantime, we are still vulnerable to the conspirators' masking attempts," stated Robert with a measure of concern.

Cheng spoke and her words echoed the years she spent with her family deceiving and second-guessing the law. "I don't think our sabotage 'friends' will try anything while the Legion is on board sniffing around. Not to mention our own heightened efforts in getting to the bottom of things with this little discovery of our science officer."

Mac put out her hands and crossed them in a rejecting motion saying, "If anyone should be credited with getting the ball rolling on our little success, it's you, Cheng. After all, we wouldn't have thought of or even known about kherzodine if you hadn't found out about it in your examination of that little puff of smoke."

"Okay," Cheng said. "We can all take some credit for this breakthrough, but I'm still amazed at how quickly you came up with a formula that would replicate the kherzodine. Doesn't that kind of research take more time?"

"Normally, yes," stated Mac. "Since I had already done hours and hours of research on alien physics dealing with the development of 'trilliatide,' I figured I would start there with the kherzodine issue. When I discovered that it worked, I was able to fly through the rest of the problem in order to reach a satisfactory conclusion."

She yawned fully as she finished, prompting Robert to say, "How much sleep did that 'quick' research allow you to get, commander?"

"Let's just say that my beauty sleep is in serious need of replenishing," stated the science officer as she tried to stifle another yawn.

He was deep in thought. *How had they discovered the new transporting technique his scientists had come up with? Blast! Now he had to alter his plans for the ambassador. Was that inept mole he had on the* Mall *starship working as a double agent feeding Mathews and his officers his plans?* He pondered over that for several seconds and thought, *No, I can't believe she has the brains or disposition to make that work. It's got to be that whiz kid, Stinson. She's got too much smarts for her own good. I might need to arrange a convenient accident for her.*

At that, he headed toward the bridge of his own starfighter to get it ready for the next phase in the destruction of the Earth's project, the starship *Cosmic Mall*.

CHAPTER FIVE

STRATEGIES

An impromptu meeting had been called by Keanyn in order to bring everyone up to date on their latest assignments. There was one difference in this meeting. Instead of using their private corner in the officers' mess, the captain felt the need for more security and convened the meeting in the council room in Robert's quarters.

Keanyn started the gathering with the following, "You all seem very anxious so I'm guessing that you have some good information for us. I know some of what you've discovered and I hope the rest is as positive. It looks as if we're getting to the end of this tangled thread that's been choking our mission for the last few weeks since the tragedy. We also need to keep our eyes on the Legion's investigators so that we're not blindsided by them. So I'll start the proceedings with the information derived from Mac concerning her idea to use Lindsey as a shadow for Dek and his team. What have you got for us, Mac?"

She started her report on a positive note saying, "First of all, Lindsey jumped at the chance to help us by keeping an eye on the 'Legion cronies,' as she calls them. She doesn't know about the full scope of our investigations. She just thinks of this as a way to know what's going on with their investigation so that we can defend ourselves if need be. Anyway, she says that Dek is determined to bring the blame for the sabotage squarely on our shoulders and that he would not be above planting or manipulating evidence to that end. Also, she said that the sixth member of their team, named Raschkit, whom she suspects is a plant from somewhere within the Legion whose duty is to not only feed info to Dek, but to relay anything he deems crippling to our mission back to the Legion."

"How did she get herself privy to such information?" asked Edward.

"If you'll remember, I told you all how Lindsey has used her feminine wiles to obtain information in the past, though not in as serious a situation as this. On this occasion, she posed as a disgruntled officer who felt snubbed by you, captain, when she tried her charms on you. She, then, said that she began to notice unusual behavior from you and our esteemed chief of security. Believe me, Dek ate that up and is all too happy to keep Lindsey close at hand where she has no trouble gathering information."

"I thought Dek was inept, but he's a gullible fool as well," stated Robert as he shook his head in disgust.

Mac continued her report. "Oh, he's all that, Robert, but the one we really need to keep our eyes on is Raschkit. He stays in the background and is often on his trans-pad, which Lindsey is sure he uses to communicate back and forth between whoever he's working for in the Legion and Commander Dek."

"Well, aside from throwing Robert and me under the bus, that was a very eye-opening report, Mac," said Keanyn with a look of amusement. He continued, "That is not the only report from our esteemed science officer. Tell us about your extraordinary findings concerning the masking technologies that our adversaries are employing."

Mac stated, "I cannot take more than a small portion of the credit for that revelation, Keanyn. Other efforts must be acknowledged. Robert used excellent questioning and ascertained from our chief engineer, Stokes, the extent to which he felt the engineering of the masking apparatus on the *Hawk* had been manipulated to allow for their transfers to this ship. He was fairly certain that it involved the speed of the transfers but couldn't figure out what they could have used as a catalyst. That idea was then brought to me to see if I could figure out a physics answer to the question. But that would have taken me a considerable amount of time with no guarantee of a proper solution."

"So what provided the answer, which appears to be one of the reasons why Keanyn called us here for this emergency meeting?" This was voiced by Grannison.

Mac, smiling broadly as she had effected the response she'd hoped for, said, "That most important part of the story must be told by our quick-minded Lieutenant Cheng Wong."

Cheng stood up with a deep blush on her face and began explaining how she had noticed small traces of the new and little-known element kherzodine in the very small puff of smoke detected by Mac and her at the moment of transfer. Then followed the full disclosure on the effect of kherzodine and Mac's subsequent experiment that now gave them the ability to not only detect the transfers from their enemies onto the *Mall* ship, but to duplicate the transfer ability themselves.

Robert was the next to speak. "It sounds like we have been making some excellent progress toward solving this case but, since Stenn is not here, I assume he is still down on Janos. Do we have any word from him, Keanyn?"

"Yes we do," proclaimed the captain. "But I caution you all not to make too much of what he has discovered so far. Even he has been reticent to apply any definitive explanation to the information."

"Please don't keep us in suspense, captain. I'm sure his mission is as dangerous as it is important," Edward spoke, and he was visibly anxious about Stenn's welfare as well as his findings.

"I, too, am concerned for his welfare," said Stenn's mother, ND. "I know I have been perceived as rather emotionless with a calculating mind, but, I assure you, I am still very much a mother where my son is concerned. Of all the espionage, subterfuge, and investigating Stenn has done, this is, by far, the most dangerous assignment he has ever undertaken. His life has been in peril before but not to the extent that, if he were discovered, he would not only pay with his life, but the safety of all of us on this ship and the ship itself would hang in the balance."

As she finished, she gathered the folds of her elegant royal blue taffeta dress around her in a motion of a butterfly going back into its chrysalis.

Keanyn spoke in a hushed and respectful tone saying, "I am sure we all appreciate your deep concern for Stenn and I can assure you that he remains safe and on his highest alert. He truly appreciates his precarious position and is prepared to make a quick escape if there is any chance of his discovery.

As to the information he has, so far, reported to me, it consists of the discovery of the *Hawk* being hidden in a secret hangar on property leased to the Saffo V diplomatic contingent." After gasps and looks of astonishment, Keanyn continued. "As remarkable as that discovery is, there is one more piece of news that eclipses it."

At this point, Keanyn paused, to make sure he had their undivided attention. After looking around the room he leaned forward putting his hands, palms down, on the table, and spoke slowly and assuredly. "Ambassador Yahnsoof Calluran is also being kept in that same hangar but it is not clear if he is a guest or a prisoner."

The room erupted in voices as the magnitude of this information hit them. Order was brought to the room by ND rising to her feet. She raised her head with her silver-streaked dark hair and her penetrating blue eyes and said, "While we do not want to jump to conclusions, as Keanyn has said, we can surmise two different paths to take. If Ambassador Calluran is a guest then he is, most likely, a conspirator in this dastardly plot and we must direct all our efforts in neutralizing his power and influence by whatever means possible."

Cheng broke in with the logical question. "And if he is a prisoner?"

"Then we must use whatever means are at our disposal to rescue him and obtain whatever information he can supply that will aid us in arriving at a successful conclusion."

At this statement from ND, Keanyn outlined a plan for both extricating Stenn from trouble if he were discovered and dealing with the situation concerning the ambassador. There were, of course, suggestions from nearly everyone on the problem of how to either silence or rescue Ambassador Calluran. In the end, it was decided to use

Stenn to discover whether the ambassador was friend or foe and use the method of transporting them back to the *Mall* ship that had been employed by their adversaries so effectively. They decided that whatever the case, they needed him alive in order to find out everything he knew or was able to find out about the sabotage plot and the plans of the saboteurs going forward.

Keanyn nervously cleared his throat as he was now about to introduce something that he knew would run up against a lot of opposition. The room got quiet as they all noticed that he was acting particularly fidgety. Keanyn rubbed his hands on his handkerchief and then wiped his moist brow off with it and spoke.

"What I am about to suggest will seem a bit daft to some, if not all, of you, but something was said by one of the members of the bridge crew which made me realize that we have been overlooking a very large section of this starship as far as clues and personnel are concerned and that is the mall itself. While it would take an astronomical amount of time to dig through the files of the more than four thousand people who work there, there is one person who knows more about the mall and the people working there — including all the little secrets they may hide — than anyone else." He paused dramatically before saying, "Saffaw!"

The room got extremely quiet as they all thought that they had misheard what Keanyn had said. It took about five seconds for them to realize they weren't hearing things after which the room's decibel level went through the roof.

"What could have possessed you to think THAT was a good idea?" shouted Grannison.

"In what universe is that a good idea!?" screamed Cheng.

Edward added, "I think it may be time for a brain scan,

Keanyn. I'm afraid something's gotten in your head and altered your thinking process!"

The commanding voice of Robert Porter cut through the cacophony of voices. "Keanyn, I believe he would be an invaluable asset to our cabal. Yes, he is a con man and has a dubious character, but he knows the nature of a swindler or someone who tries to hide what they are. On the plus side, he is devoted to the success of the *Mall's* mission and has proven to be an excellent manager despite his flaws. The help he could give to us would be immeasurable. I only regret I hadn't thought of it before you did!"

Whatever further objections the others had ready to voice were squelched by Robert's endorsement of Saffaw. As they all thought about it, the reasonableness of his argument began to dawn on them.

It was agreed that Saffaw should be approached to see if he would help them. One bit of advice was included as to who should handle the matter. It was felt that Robert, not Keanyn, should be the one to work with their Raushdonian mall manager. Keanyn fully agreed that Robert was the right man for the job.

Everyone except Keanyn, ND, and Edward now prepared to leave the conference room but the captain held up his right hand in a gesture indicating that they weren't quite finished. As they all stopped their departure preparations, they looked at him with questioning faces. He answered their stares with, "I know you are all anxious to get on with your duties, but you are forgetting that Edward, ND, and I had the task of trying to further jog Salfrod's memory using the 'put him back in the same place' method and you might like to know what we found out."

"Yes, we would," stated Grannison, as they all sat back down. "I'm sorry but we all somehow forgot about you three trying to delve back into Salfrod's mind. I think the news concerning Saffaw, the ambassador, and Stenn's harrowing mission has gotten us all ready for action and we couldn't wait to get started." The others all agreed.

Keanyn smiled and said, "I fully understand but what we were able to help our congenial stowaway remember is going to put a twist on this investigation that threw us for a loop and will, no doubt, have the same effect on you."

If any of them were fidgeting to get back to their investigations, they were now riveted to the next words that Keanyn uttered. When he finished, they all were dumbfounded, uttering expressions like, "That can't be possible!" "I don't believe it!" "Is he sure of that?" "His memory must be faulty!"

Keanyn calmed them down and assured them. "We ran him through the scenario half a dozen times and his memory of the person who met him in the shuttle and gave him that terrible blow to his head was the same. It also underscores the need for us to look very closely at the mall staff."

With all of them agreeing, even more, to the use of Saffaw in examining the personnel working at the mall, they hoped they hadn't waited too long to start looking.

As they filed out of the conference room, Grannison made his way to the side of the captain and addressed that very issue with him. "Why were we all so blind to the need for our investigations to cover the mall and the possibility that someone there might be involved in the sabotage plot?"

Keanyn replied, "I think that since all of us are part of the military aspect of this ship and we have very little to do with the mall itself, aside from shopping or other use of our leisure time, we just didn't see it as a threat. Of all of us, Cheng has the closest ties to the activity inside the mall, but her attention was mainly on the shuttle bay since that was where Salfrod was found."

"I suppose you're right, but that doesn't excuse all of us missing that vital point," noted Grannison with a frustrated expression. He began stroking his van dyke beard as if in thought and added, "I was, like the rest, perplexed and alarmed at your suggestion of adding Saffaw to our team initially. With Robert's insight and the apparent need to look into the mall staff, I feel that our clever mall manager's unique skills will be most welcome."

"As valuable as Saffaw may prove to be, he will still need to be kept on a short chain," remarked Keanyn with a look of concerned amusement.

Grannison said, "And there is not a better person to monitor him than our chief of security, Robert Porter."

Just at that moment, a crewman from the bridge raced up to the two officers, stopped abruptly, saluted, and said, "Excuse me, sirs, but there is an urgent need for you to go to the shuttle bay. Lieutenant Philpot received a communication from Janos that General Beckton has arrived from the planet's surface."

"How very clever of the communication officer and much appreciated as well," observed Grannison Loche. Turning to the captain he added, "I didn't even know the general had left Earth in the first place. Were you aware of his presence on Janos, Keanyn?"

Keanyn's response was, "I had a suspicion that there was an investigative entourage from Earth on the planet, but the general as a member and probable head of that team was not known to me. You see, Grann, in part of Stenn's last report I received just before our meeting, it mentioned that a small group of Legion officials had just arrived on Janos. He was not able to get the identity of any of the individuals, though."

Grannison's reaction to this news was, "Well, that's all we need! Another Legion investigation we need to keep our eyes on!"

"I'm not so sure about that," replied Keanyn. "If it was anyone but the general, I would be extremely concerned. But General Beckton has been an ally of mine for some time and I can't see him coming all the way to Janos to undermine our efforts or accuse us of any wrongdoing."

"I hope you're right about that, captain. Personally, I'm very worried."

CHAPTER SIX

PICKING SAFFAW'S BRAIN

General Anthony Beckton was anxiously awaiting Keanyn as he arrived at his quarters following the close of their group's latest meeting. The general appeared calm but the subtle tapping of his right foot revealed his nervous expectation. They sat at the well-stocked bar in the captain's quarters. He began by saying, "Whatever you and your fellow officers were discussing must have been so important that you couldn't be on the bridge to greet a superior officer as he came on board."

Keanyn Mathews knew that, while Beckton was citing a major protocol faux pas on the captain's part, the general was probably not overly concerned about it. His anxiety at having to wait for Keanyn was more likely due to whatever news he had for the captain and any he hoped to receive from him.

"My sincere apologies, sir," said Keanyn. "But you are correct in guessing that my delay was due to some important information that a number of my officers have discovered concerning the sabotage plot. I might also add that Legion headquarters failed to inform me that a group of investigators from Earth was on the surface of Janos in addition to those on board my ship. And I was just informed by my communications officer that you, sir, were among them and had been transported to this vessel."

"Yes," remarked the general in a thoughtful tone. "It seems that the internal affairs division convinced the interplanetary investigative department that they should head up the investigation of the A Deck sabotage. Someone in that division still has a glitch in their hard drive concerning the *Mall* starship and they are itching to discredit this project at any cost. They've convinced several prominent individuals in the Legion to not only allow IA to lead the sabotage investigations but to communicate as little as possible to any officer or crew member of this ship. If I hadn't called in some favors, I wouldn't have been able to get a team of my own together to give you some help. Though the Legion thinks that I felt that a team investigating on the planet's surface was necessary." As he concluded, he looked at Keanyn with a knowing twinkle in his eye. "However, I learned enough about you in all those years of observing you before, during, and after your training, that you've already got someone down on the surface doing some intensive investigating already."

Keanyn smiled as he answered General Beckton, "General, I can't get anything past you. As a matter of fact, I sent ND's son, Stenn, down. He is a top-notch covert operative and has uncovered some interesting facts. But he is only one man and I am greatly relieved to know that you are here and intend to help us."

General Beckton looked concerned as he added to his previous comments, "I don't like the fact that there are those in IA with enough ill will toward the *Mall* project and with enough power and influence to manipulate this investigation. It makes me suspicious that they could have something to do with the sabotage itself."

"I was thinking the same thing, sir," said Keanyn, as the information had been revealed to him. "I'm also wondering if those 'influential' persons in IA might also have a connection to Saffo V which seems to sit at the heart of this insidious conspiracy."

The general glanced intently at the ship's captain and remarked sharply. "Having recently received the information concerning Ambassador Calluran's disappearance as well as other tidbits linked to his home planet, I think it would be a good idea if you filled me in on all of your detective activities if you want my full help and cooperation. I imagine you've assembled a team?"

"If I could have accessed you, sir, I would have loved to have had your input," said Keanyn who proceeded to fill the general in on what they had discovered.

"You've had a lot to deal with, Keanyn," said Beckton. "I don't think I would have handled it much differently. As I've said before, you are so much like I was at your age. The big difference is that, when I was your age, I wasn't the captain of a starship facing the situation that confronts you. But if we put our two heads together, maybe we can figure out where we should go from here."

Keanyn smiled knowingly as he said, "I couldn't agree more, so why don't we put our heads together and see if we can come up with a solution to our problem."

This was a statement rather than a question and General Beckton was more than happy to cooperate.

They spent the next several hours discussing strategy.

Down on the planet, Stenn was carefully following two crewmen from a supply ship that had just docked at the Janovian embassy port of Saffo V. Supply ships docking at embassy ports was not an unusual occurrence, but this one was from the Saffo V defense depot known as "Rhaakvule Symbisos."

Translated, it meant "Fortress of Trust."

Those ships commonly have their logo of a bronze shield emblazoned with a silver watchtower on the top half and crossed blue and gold laser cannons on the bottom half. Just above the shield, in a half-moon curve, is the Saffo Vian word for protect, "Meegrond." This ship had no such identification.

So, how did Stenn know it was from the defense depot? He had employed several informants in the Saffo V embassy and other info-gathering entities on Janos. After all, what kind of an espionage agent would he be if he hadn't?

The two crewmen he was following had just slipped quietly into a transpod and Stenn had to move fast to hail another pod before they gave him the slip.

Are they aware that I'm following them? he thought to himself. *If they are then I'm seriously losing my touch. But I don't think so. I'm willing to bet they don't want to be noticed or followed by anyone, and not me in particular,* he reassured himself.

After a short five-minute ride, he instructed the pod driver to let him off in front of a Janovian hunting outfitter's shop which Stenn knew was a front for a clandestine spy ring of disgruntled espionage agents from around the galaxy. His two crewmen had just been admitted inside after flashing some kind of ID. Stenn would have to find some alternative way in.

Beckton was particularly concerned about the activities of Stenn. Since he was so close to the situation on the planet, he appreciated the dangerous position that confronted Stenn.

Keanyn agreed and said that he would immediately contact Stenn to see if he felt it was a good idea as well.

"I need to get back down to the surface and fill my team in on our plan," remarked the general. I'm sure they'll have some suggestions that will prove to be valuable. I was able to recruit a pretty savvy group of associates for this operation and I know their input will be first class." He paused before leaving the room and turned back to address Keanyn. "This idea of consulting Saffaw has me a bit concerned. I interviewed him extensively before giving my approval to assign him as the mall manager and, while he is a hard worker and a go-getter, his methods of going and getting are a bit unorthodox, to say the least. The trust issue is something I question seriously."

"As do I," stated Keanyn. "In fact, I was quite hesitant in bringing it up at our meeting fearing the backlash I would receive from everyone. But the positive response I got from Robert Porter squelched any further protests the others were ready to express. Robert has a lot of experience dealing with con artists and fast talkers so we all agreed that he should be the one to handle the recruiting of Saffaw into our team. In fact, I believe he's scheduled to talk to him right now!"

"While I'm flattered that you've considered including me on your investigative team, Lieutenant Commander Porter. I'm surprised that you would choose someone of my, shall we say, unusual reputation. While I pride myself on uncovering useful information about people and their circumstances, what I find out doesn't exactly coincide with the reasons you're requesting my services," remarked the loquacious Suffaw.

Robert Porter, who had arranged to meet the mall manager at one of the mall's more secluded seating areas, said, "Actually, Suffaw, your exceptional skill for digging up information could prove to be invaluable to our investigation. You see, we have been able to uncover a number of useful clues and information that have helped us to piece together a trail to solving the sinister sabotage plot. We have concentrated all of our efforts on the military and political areas. We realized that we had totally ignored the mall personnel in the mix."

"I can see how you would have overlooked that area in your investigations, Robert—if I may call you by your first name." Suffaw continued, "But I can tell you that there is enough intrigue to be found in the behind-the-scenes activities of the mall staff, both management and employees, to reveal any number of conspiracies. While these plots are generally confined to competitive retail espionage or efforts to exact revenge from perceived injustices, like you, I've never looked at them as having a military or political motive." He paused as his mind was bringing back certain occurrences. "But, now that I think about it, one or two of those little plots could have had another motive besides the usual ones."

Robert Porter looked sharply at Saffaw and asked with curiosity in his voice. "What kind of motives are you talking about?"

"Well," said Saffaw, "It has to do with the people and the places they came from that aroused my suspicions at the time."

"You mean that you've had these suspicions all along and never thought to pursue them or inform, say, Mrs. Pickle or even me and my colleagues?" said Robert a bit incredulously. "We could have found something that was very important to our investigations."

"Now hold on, Robert!" exclaimed the mall manager. "I did, in fact, say something to Mrs. Pickle about the incidences but she was so busy and distracted with an upcoming VIP visit that she told me it was probably nothing or had something to do with the preparations she was dealing with as well." Saffaw paused, squinted his eyes, looked resolutely at the head of security, and continued. "When I don't have to deal with our bombastic owner over an issue that involves the activity of any of the mall personnel, I gladly comply. She dismissed my suspicions and I was more than happy to forget them and move ahead with my normal duties. Besides, by informing her I conveniently covered my behind so that if anything did come from the situations, I could remind her that I had informed her and she had told me to forget it."

"That's called 'passing the buck' you know?" stated Robert. "But that's your MO to avoid consequences, I believe."

Saffaw feigned a hurtful expression and whined, "Really, Lieutenant Porter, I am deeply crushed that you would accuse me of avoiding responsibility. My previous statement was meant to convey the thought that I did not want to disobey the order of my employer so I simply did not pursue my inquiries any further."

Robert was not about to take the bait and get into a philosophical debate about the intent of expressions with

Saffaw. He just said, "Well, it's all just a moot point now, anyway. Since you couldn't pursue the matter any further with Mrs. Pickle, perhaps you would like to tell me what these incidents were. I will defer any backlash that may come from Mrs. Pickle if she should learn of our investigations."

"I'm happy to hear that," remarked Saffaw and added, "It's a challenge just to stay a step ahead of her in our normal dealings, much less play the mind games that would be necessary if we were dealing with an unusual situation that could carry interplanetary consequences."

"Good," said Robert. "Now, do you think you could tell me about these incidences?"

Saffaw began by saying, "The reason these occurrences struck me as unusual was, as I said before, the people who were involved and the source of the information." He scratched his excessively furry head with his unusually long right arm and continued. "The first incident came from our head of horticultural sciences for the *Mall*, Stella Steel. She remarked to me that her assistant—the Sharlee, Larindo kwark—was acting a bit unusual."

Robert interrupted, "Aren't they the ones who do the plant and flower arrangements in the mall?"

"Precisely!" said Saffaw. "But there's much more to it than that. Ms. Steel has a doctorate and Larindo has a master's in botany, and they apply their skills most diligently to the proper way to display those plants and flowers and what specific varieties will survive and thrive in the particular climate that exists in the mall. In fact, they are also in charge of climate control within the mall. In fact," he continued. "You surely noticed their skills when those two disgruntled janitors crashed that cruise mod into the waterfall display?"

Robert nodded his head as he said, "Of course I noticed

the skillful and swift way in which that situation was gotten under control, but I didn't realize that the two botanists were responsible. But isn't Ms. kwark a Sharlee?"

"Indeed she is," returned Saffaw. "But that doesn't mean she isn't intelligent. She is a most skillful botanist as well as a quick thinker." He returned to the subject at hand by noting. "You are, obviously, familiar with the predominant attitude of mirth that makes up the disposition of Sharlees?" When Robert nodded he continued, "Therefore, when Ms. Steel reported that Ms. kwark had been moody and a bit depressed, I was surprised. I asked her what she thought accounted for this unusual behavior on the Sharlee's part. When she said that it might be coming from some of the plants, I asked her if it was a specific plant or plants. Her response was to shake her head and say that it was probably just her imagination and she departed."

"Why do you think she so quickly changed her direction and ended the conversation?" asked Robert.

Saffaw replied with a concerned look. "I'm not sure, but I can tell you that her abruptness at ending our discussion caused me as much concern as the information she had given me in the first place."

Robert Porter continued trying to get as much information from Saffaw as he could. He knew that, in dealing with the mall manager, he would need to keep pressing him for details due to the fact that Saffaw was so reluctant to give up any information he received or suspicions he might have. Saying too much could give up any leverage he may have had over the people involved and he didn't like to lose that control.

So he asked him, "Did you have some specific ideas or suspicions?"

Saffaw's reply was protective. "My thoughts were not

anything remotely connected to the lines of inquiry you and your colleagues have been concerned with, Robert. They were more along the lines of what were these two trying to hide from me. Was this a set up to get around me by using a red herring or to get something from me?"

Robert wasn't going to let Saffaw get away with that deception and straightforwardly said, "If you are going to be a contributing member of this investigation, Saffaw, you are going to have to sacrifice some of your behind-the-scenes subterfuge. It may lessen your influence to a degree but there are much larger issues at stake. Remember, we've had to sacrifice our own reservations to include you on our team."

Saffaw said, "I'm sorry. It's just that it's so hard for me to trust someone so openly with my thoughts after all these years of making sure that people don't really know what I'm up to. I admit that my motives are selfish to a degree, but I've never done so just to hurt or discredit someone. I might be selfish but I'm not spiteful. If my actions have truly hurt some it's been either unintentional or deserving due to their underhanded and/or malicious behavior. Any of those I unintentionally hurt were compensated in some way later."

As Saffaw spoke, Robert realized how difficult it must be for him to bare his feelings like this. In all of Robert's dealings with con artists and the like, he had never known of even one who had openly admitted to such feelings. All of a sudden a thought flashed into his head and he said, "I remember an incident right after our first port of call when a clerk in one of the jewelry stores was exposed when selling a certain brooch made from genuine speldane from Corsrun in the Ursa Minor system. It was learned later that the store manager was blackmailing her for a very small indiscretion on her part. I think she claimed she had completed her schooling in alien gemology when she hadn't quite finished her final year. The result of your revelations concerning her was the loss of her job, and her unceremonious ouster from this ship to the planet we were serving with no fee to return to Earth, her home planet. When the full truth was learned she, somehow, landed a position as assistant manager for the main competitor of her previous employer and her expertise as a gemologist earned her an honorary degree and totally discredited her former manager. That was your doing?"

"I merely got the ball rolling and monitored her progress," said Saffaw with no hint of false modesty.

"I dare say you did a lot more than that!" exclaimed Robert. He looked thoughtfully at Saffaw and noted, "I can see that there are more layers to you than I had previously been aware. You, my friend, are something I have never seen in the world of deception. A con man with honor."

The Raushdonian was all smiles and a deep blush as he said, "Why, Lieutenant Porter, I believe that was the most gracious left-handed compliment I have ever received. While it has been oft quoted that 'there is no honor among thieves,' I intend to change that to 'thieves can be honorable.'"

As they settled into a comfortable easiness Robert brought Saffaw's attention back to their former discussion. "You had mentioned that there was more than one incident that aroused your suspicions. What was that?"

"Well, I'm beginning to think that this wasn't a separate incident but, rather, an extension of the first." This statement caused Robert to pay even more attention to Saffaw's story.

"About a week later, Larindo kwark herself came to me and asked if I would consider hiring a number of her Sharlee friends for positions in custodial, security areas and as assistants to her and Stella in the transporting of the large and heavy quantities of plants, trees, soil, and the like needed for their work in keeping the mall a beautiful garden atmosphere. Though this seemed an unusual request at first, I did see the practical aspect of using the strength of Sharlees in jobs that required a good bit of heavy activity. They had been relying on Larindo and a small staff of workers from a variety of planets but, it seemed, that most of them had transferred to other areas of the mall or returned to their home planets so their need for more help appeared justified."

Robert looked inquisitively at Saffaw and asked, "Was there something else about all that that seemed strange to you?"

"Not at first," replied Saffaw. "A few days after this request, I was making arrangements to hire the extra Sharlees when I discovered that a couple of them had gone out of their way to strong-arm several of the helpers to transfer off the ship rather than voluntarily depart. This intimidation caused the rest of them to take positions in other areas of the mall."

"Did you still hire the Sharlees anyway?" Robert asked with concern.

Saffaw answered with a cunning grin. "Remember who you're talking to, Robert. My inquisitiveness coupled with my suspicious nature caused me to desire to get to the bottom of this deception so I went ahead and hired some eleven Sharlees. Three in security—once I ran it by your assistant Ross Carter and received his approval—four in custodial, and four as laborers to help Stella and Larindo."

Robert was digesting this information when, at the mention of Ross Carter, he sat up and declared, "I was never made known of Ross's agreeing to that! He's usually good about informing me when he has to make a tricky decision like that."

Saffaw sheepishly replied, "That could be because he didn't know there was anything unusual about the hire since I didn't inform him of the suspicious circumstances. I presented it to him as a need for the extra muscle because the loads of very heavy products had increased and one Sharlee just wasn't enough to handle it all, and since the security had been stepped up because of the suspected sabotage, we might as well beef up our security in the mall as well. There was no reason for him to suspect anything more than that."

"I have given Ross a fair amount of independence in how he sees to the security in the mall," said Robert. "He is only to check with me if there is something out of the norm, and this probably didn't seem unusual to him. Still, I think I'll have a talk with him about reporting to me regularly. That should help keep things from slipping through the cracks." He looked sharply at the Raushdonian manipulator, pointed his finger at him, and sternly reproved him saying, "This is just another example of how you are going to have to be open and honest with us as a member of our team. We want you to use some of your 'unique' skills in helping us to get to the bottom of the plots of the saboteurs but you need to shed the scheming and subterfuge when informing us of what you find. Do you honestly feel you can do that?"

This was a tense moment for both of them. Robert was anxious for Saffaw's answer and Saffaw was deeply searching his heart to see if he could answer in the affirmative. After a good thirty seconds, he replied, "What is that saying you have on Earth? Ah, yes. 'A leopard doesn't change his spots.' Well, I'm not a leopard and I don't have spots, so I think I can truly make changes. I want this mission of the *Mall* starship to succeed and if that means I need to change, then so be it!"

His emphatic response was a real encouragement to Robert, who had too often witnessed the seedy underbelly of mankind and even aliens. He had to constantly fight against developing a cynical attitude, which was not healthy for one so young.

The two of them spent the next hour and a half discussing situations Saffaw had uncovered but none of them came up to the interest of the "Botany Bunch," as they came to call it. After their discussion, it was decided that they needed to meet with the entire investigative group ASAP.

That is why, by 0800 hours the next morning, they were all gathered in Robert's quarters to discuss the latest strategy. Keanyn had appointed Robert to chair the meeting as he would be contributing most of the latest information as well as introducing Saffaw to the group.

"I'm aware that you all know our affable mall manager, Saffaw, but I have discovered some additional layers to his personality I think you will come to appreciate as I have," began Robert as he opened the meeting. "We have discussed several curious incidents, two of which really piqued my interest because they tend to confirm the seemingly out-of-character information we had received concerning the Sharlees on board this vessel." At this, there arose surprised murmurs from most of the others. Robert waited until their reaction subsided acknowledging it with a subtle nod of his head.

"I was as flabbergasted as you were when we initially received the reports of their unusual behavior," he spoke again. "But what Saffaw has reported to me is in line with what we heard. There seems to be some bizarre twist to their normally jocular personality, as well as a little discontent being displayed by a few of them. Our own Larindo kwark for one."

At this point, Keanyn interjected a question. "Robert, have you come up with any theories or ideas as to how their strange behavior came about? I, for one, have an idea but I can't substantiate it."

Many of the others declared that they had been thinking about the same thing and started voicing their opinions simultaneously. The cacophony of voices was quickly terminated by Robert saying, "ONE AT A TIME! We won't get to a conclusion by talking all at once!"

The room became quiet then some subdued statements of apology were uttered.

All eyes were on Keanyn as he began, "As I said, I don't have any proof but I have based my theory on a logical train of thought that seems plausible. It seems to me that there is an X factor in this conspiracy/sabotage equation that needs to be identified. We all agree that the source of our problem emanates from Saffo V." A quiet chorus of agreement followed. "We have also recently learned that Ambassador Calluran is either staying or being held in the Saffo V embassy on Janos," he continued. "The Saffo Vian ambassador to Janos, Iamlaurie Musslavo, has been revealed as a former espionage operative from the Saffo V Security Force."

When Keanyn noted the surprised expressions nearly everyone else in the room had after his last statement, he smiled at the reaction he was hoping for and explained.

"I must apologize for inserting that little tidbit into the proceedings, but I had received a report from Stenn that he had uncovered that fact just before I came to this meeting. I believe ND and Robert were the only others that were aware of that." He received affirmative nods from them.

Keanyn went on, "Stenn believes Ambassador Musslavo is being used to facilitate certain undercover activities dealing with the continued efforts by our enemies to discredit the effectiveness of our mission. He is not certain who or from where the ambassador is receiving his instructions but I think I can make a pretty good guess and that guess constitutes our X factor.

"There is someone who has been directing this entire conspiracy from the beginning. It is his brainchild and stems from a perceived notion that he has been discredited and disrespected by the authorities of Saffo V as well as his own family. He also shares feelings of disgust for— what is in the eyes of most critics—the frivolous nature of the Earth's contribution to this very vessel, the starship *Cosmic Mall*. Therefore, he is determined to thwart this project at all costs!"

The room was now abuzz with chatter as its occupants both questioned who this person was and who they thought it might be. Attempts to bring things back to order took several minutes but, finally, the room settled and Robert began asserting his chairmanship once again. He stood up to get everyone's attention, cleared his throat, and scanned the room to be sure all eyes were on him. His voice was both firm and confident as he spoke.

"I believe I am following you correctly, Keanyn, when I say that I have suspected this person as our chief antagonist for some time. Hearing you cite the reasons you feel he is this X factor has solidified my own suspicions. It also may shed light on whether Ambassador Calluran is involved in the saboteurs' plots, for, if I guess correctly, you do not think that the ambassador is this X factor."

Keanyn nodded affirmatively as he motioned for the security chief to continue.

"I also think that you began to piece this together after you heard about Ambassador Calluran's comment about ungrateful relations a few weeks ago. I too found that comment odd and felt that there was something sinister behind it. It is totally out of character for the ambassador to be so distracted as to fail to acknowledge the greeting of another individual, and then to appear so upset by what appears to be a family problem that he expressed his frustration loud enough to be heard by someone close shows that he was so distracted he didn't even perceive that anyone else was there!"

After shaking his head and looking concerned, Robert looked at Keanyn and said, "Am I right?"

The captain's reply was to look at Robert with an amused expression and say, "My dear, Robert. I don't know whether to be flattered or afraid that our minds think along the same lines." He continued, "That comment of Ambassador Calluran has bothered me greatly ever since Edward told us about it. The ambassador has always been good about departmentalizing his thoughts and keeping any personal issues from interfering with his duties. So for him to reveal any frustration he has outside of his functions on this ship is not only unusual but even alarming."

At this time, Mac spoke up and expressed what everyone else was thinking. "Keanyn, you and Robert may be in agreement as to the identity of this X factor manipulator, but the rest of us—with the possible exception of ND—have no clue. How about letting us in on it?"

"If I might answer that," said Robert. He received the go-ahead from Keanyn and continued. "Who is the only family member we know of that has been involved with

Ambassador Calluran since our mission began? Whose ship was involved with the transporting of our, now, beloved stowaway Salfrod? And whose crew has been using a highly efficient form of transporting from that ship to this one?" Before anyone could steal his thunder by replying Robert said, "Why, the ambassador's own nephew Ansmed! If you will remember, he has a long history of criminal activity and rebellion. He was incarcerated, and when he was released, he declared himself reformed but did speak out against the Earth's contribution to the Legion and expressed disappointment when his uncle eventually accepted and embraced the idea of the *Cosmic Mall*.

"He used his connections with his uncle to take his ship out of mothballs, and then retooled it with some of the most cutting-edge engineering and technology, which, no doubt, included the upgraded transport system. If he just wanted to have his old ship back, he would have been content to make some repairs and normal updates and leave it at that. But he turned the *Hawk* into a sleek, state-of-the-art interstellar starship and recruited a crew of, what appears to be, first-rate mercenaries. That smells wrong to me."

As the others mulled this over, ND added a comment, "Saffaw, I believe the Frothy Mug pub run by your cousin has been used as the location where the crew of the *Hawk* has transported from on this ship. Would you care to elaborate?"

The Raushdonian mall manager was not put off by her question and proceeded to answer quite freely. It seems that he was fully embracing the new persona Robert had encouraged him to develop. His reply to ND began with full acknowledgment of his cousin's involvement. "I was aware of my cousin Hammfruul's arrangement with the crew of the *Hawk*. Of course, we both looked at it as a fairly lucrative business deal and not some undercover attempt to gain access to this ship as part of the sabotage plot. Remember, no one from either the ship's command staff or any of us on the mall staff were giving any serious consideration to the mall as part of the conspiracy once it had been eliminated as a target for the saboteurs. And as you remember, that occurred fairly early in the mission."

Robert interjected, "It still bothers me that even after we became aware of the transporting of the *Hawk's* personnel to this ship and the subsequent departure of Ambassador Calluran through the Frothy Mug, we failed to focus on the mall. But we're aggressively working to correct that."

Saffaw took up the narrative again. "Despite whatever oversights may have occurred, we now have an opportunity to correct them. I will get with my cousin and discreetly encourage him to pay more attention to the transporting of the crew of the *Hawk* and to keep me informed of any details related to it. You may be aware of when it occurs, but I can find out the particulars."

"Very good," said Robert.

Just at that moment, Keanyn's personal com alerted him of a message from JA. "Captain, I have just received an urgent communication from General Beckton on the planet. He says that something appears to be going on at the Saffo V embassy on Janos. He says that his group has been working closely with Stenn and that he, Stenn, has decided to get into the embassy to learn what's going on. The general fervently discouraged him but Stenn was determined and got into the embassy under cover."

Keanyn informed the rest of the group of this alarming development. He got back to JA on the com and gave him directions to contact the general and find out as much as possible as to what was happening at that embassy, then turned his attention back to those in Robert's quarters.

ND was especially adamant that she should go down to the planet and help General Beckton and his group to monitor Stenn's activity, if possible. They agreed and Keanyn commented, "Well, we had better be ready for action because things are beginning to move at a fast pace!"

CHAPTER SEVEN

AN IMPORTANT DISCOVERY

Before anyone could be transported down to the planet, Keanyn had Robert, ND, and Grannison meet him in his quarters. He didn't want ND or any others he might send down to Janos to go there with no organized plan, and he wanted to make certain that he was aware of that plan and would be kept abreast of how it was proceeding.

He started by saying, "ND, I know you are a professional, but seeing how your son has put himself in harm's way, I want to be sure that your emotions won't cloud your judgment."

"Captain," she began. "I can assure you that Stenn has been in similar circumstances before and I have gone to his aid. The situation has always been resolved without any familial sentiments affecting the outcome." She appeared to be her usual calm and confident self as she looked Keanyn right in the eyes, but he thought he detected a gleam of worry in those dark blue orbs.

"That's good to hear," he said knowing any statement expressing doubt would be insulting to her. He continued, "I would like to ask what you and Robert plan to do while on Janos. For instance, how will you proceed to locate and then make contact with Stenn—assuming you are able to do so? Also what ideas you might have for rescuing him, if need be, and doing all of this without raising any alarms."

Robert and ND were looking at Keanyn with some confusion as Robert spoke up. "Keanyn, I wasn't aware that you were sending me down to the planet with ND. I think that would put too many of us at risk and I believe I am vitally needed on board this ship to oversee the security here."

ND shook her head and said, "My presence, as well as General Beckton and his team, should more than suffice to handle any problems. Add to that the fact that if Stenn is not hindered by captivity or something worse, he will be using his many skills to uncover needed information."

"I didn't mean to suggest that Robert go down to the planet with you, ND. I was merely noting that given the fact that you two have often worked closely together on many investigations that this would be one in which you would collaborate again, with one on the planet and the other on the ship," corrected Keanyn.

"Well, of course, we'll be doing that!" exclaimed Robert.

"Then I would like to know how you will be proceeding," said the captain. "I just wanted to see how alert you were. You're going to need all of your antenna operating at a high level to make sure you don't miss anything during this operation."

Robert replied, "I'm all too aware of that, and that is why ND and I must communicate in a highly secretive code during her time on the planet."

Grannison suddenly chimed in. "Before you start talking about Robert and ND's plans, I would like to know why you asked me to be here, Keanyn. I see no reason to include me in deep espionage discussions unless the addition of a pilot is key to your plans."

"As a matter of fact, you're not far off, Grann," stated Keanyn. "I don't think that we want to introduce ND to the planet in a clandestine manner. I think it would serve our purpose better if her presence on Janos was obvious—and that's where you come in."

It was now time for ND to question the captain's maneuvers and her perplexity was evident in her voice. "What! Do you plan to have Grannison fly me down to the surface without even the normal procedure of transporting, and then I just walk around on Janos as if to say 'Here I am'?"

"Precisely!" stated Keanyn.

"I think I see the method to his madness, ND," injected Robert. He added, "The complete transparency of your visit will keep the conspirators in the embassy from trying anything underhanded to stop you from, at least, performing some attempts at getting to the bottom of what they're up to."

"You're exactly right, Robert," stated Keanyn. "And if my diplomatic skills are still intact, I believe that it is customary for an emissary from a docked ship who is visiting any government facilities on the planet, including foreign embassies, to arrive on the planet aboard a shuttle vessel and not via transport as that would be considered an insult."

ND was now more incredulous than before as she spoke, "Now you're making me a diplomatic emissary? What's next? Will I be breaking out in song and dance for the entertainment of the embassy staff?"

Keanyn put the index finger of his right hand up to his temple and said, "Now, there's a twist I hadn't thought of. That may have some merit." His broad smile made it clear that he was not serious.

As ND indicated by her scowl that she did not appreciate Keanyn's light-hearted statement, Robert again broke in, "You have asked ND and me what our plans for her time on Janos would include. It seems as if you've already come up with some of your own, captain."

Grannison stated, "Since I have been the pilot on many diplomatic missions, Keanyn is exactly right that it is considered diplomatic protocol to arrive on the planet to which you are making your visit by either starship—if the planet has facilities large enough to accommodate them—or shuttle and not by transport. And let me add my guess that by ND making a diplomatic visit to the Saffo V embassy, she will more easily be able to gain access to certain departments within the embassy." He held up a finger as if to say, *Wait! I just had a thought*, and continued, "Let me guess. She will be coming as a representative of the security division of this ship in order to speak with the Saffo V ambassador concerning the disappearance of Ambassador Calluran so as to give them a full report and ask for any assistance they can give. How's that?"

"It's like you were reading my mind, Grann," said Keanyn with respect for the quick thinking ability of Grannison Loche.

A keen awareness was now dawning on both ND and Robert's faces, it was ND who now spoke. "Captain, my hat is off to you and I am a bit ashamed to realize that my abilities as a clandestine investigator completely failed me just now. I think I need to concede that my concern for Stenn has affected me."

"No shame in that," reassured Robert. "After all, you're a mother first and an investigator second. I must admit to being a bit lost as to your intentions, Keanyn. I couldn't see how ND would accomplish anything by being transparent, as it were. But now I begin to realize that some things might be accomplished by being more open rather than being undercover and subtle."

Keanyn noted, "Subtlety will still be much needed, Robert. ND will be walking a fine line between openness and subterfuge." He then turned to Grann and said, "Let's check with Cheng on a shuttle."

Cheng Wong was busily checking each of the ten shuttle craft currently occupying the shuttle deck when Keanyn and the other three entered. She was a little surprised at their appearance as she thought that ND would have already been transported down to the planet. She spoke with some question in her voice, even though she was making a statement.

"I see that ND is still here and, even more, I wouldn't have expected any of you here on the shuttle deck at this time."

Keanyn spoke with assurance. "We have plans that require the use of one of your well-maintained shuttles, Cheng. Commander Loche will be taking ND to Janos on an important diplomatic mission."

"Apparently, that is some use of the word diplomatic to which I am not familiar, captain," said Cheng with a somewhat perplexed but amused look.

Robert spoke up, "There are many nuances in the world

of diplomacy, lieutenant. We in security are often used for the more obscure varieties. Come to think of it, my family would employ some of those obscure forms of diplomacy when we were confronted by, shall we say, certain 'officials' of the government during our family business dealings. It worked well on most occasions but not every time."

Geannison, who had moved away from the group to examine a nearby shuttle-craft, turned back and addressed Cheng, "This shuttle, the *Armstrong*, looks to be a sleek little piece of work. Might we take it on our trip to Janos, Cheng?"

"You have a wonderful eye for quality, Commander Loche. If it will just be the four of you going down to the planet, you couldn't have picked a better craft. It is not only perfect for smaller groups but its appearance says both speed and elegance."

"Actually, only ND will be riding with Grannison," stated Keanyn. "Robert and I need to remain on board. We had just finished discussing our strategy so were already together when we headed here."

"I see," said Cheng. "And will you be informing the rest of our group as to the details of that strategy, sir?"

"In due time, Cheng," stated the captain somewhat bluntly.

"Must be pretty hush-hush stuff if the rest of the investigative group isn't privy to it," declared Cheng.

Keanyn responded with assurance, "This operation is so delicate that it's as if it's walking a tightrope between success and failure. So the fewer who know about it, the better its chance for success. There is one thing you need to know, Cheng. ND is going to Janos openly as a diplomat, therefore, any support you can give her with the use of this shuttle will lend credence to her mission."

Cheng looked thoughtful as she meditated on how she could accomplish this task. Suddenly she said. "I happen to have some diplomatic paraphernalia that I could, slightly, alter and make our little shuttle appear quite official."

"That's just the kind of thing I was hoping for from you, lieutenant," said Keanyn as he cleared his throat and added, "I won't ask how you came by that paraphernalia, but I'm sure you used some of your old 'family' skills to obtain it."

"Old habits are hard to break," she said with a smirk. "Besides, I wanted to see if I had lost any of my touch."

"And what is your conclusion?" Robert asked.

Cheng looked at Robert as if he had asked a very dumb question and replied. "Really, commander, it proved to be so easy that taking candy from a baby would be an impossible task by comparison."

On the bridge of the *Mall* starship, Mac Stinson was confronted by a challenge just presented to her by Edward Butler in his capacity as alternate navigator. His question to her was, "I know that we have improved on the *Hawk's* ability to transport undetected by making the transport even faster. But can that same process be applied to larger objects like a starship?"

This had stopped Mac in her tracks, so to speak, and she responded with incredulity.

"You are suggesting a rather unheard-of task, Edward. Some experiments have been carried out on small shuttles with limited success, but nothing so large as a starship has ever been imagined, let alone attempted. May I ask what prompted this question?"

"As you probably know, I am an avid reader of twentieth

and twenty-first-century science fiction novels. There were a lot of theories and what was then considered fanciful ideas have become reality," said Edward. "The idea of transporting individuals instantly from one place to another was one of them, and look where we are now." He paused and Mac interjected a comment.

"I've read a few of those stories as well, Edward, and there do seem to be a lot of science fiction ideas that have become fact here in the twenty-third century. But that is really just the natural progression of things. You can go all the way back to Leonardo da Vinci's time and discover ideas he proposed that came about several hundred years later."

"That's true," continued Edward, "So, why can't we continue that progression now?"

Mac had a very curious smile. "I know you have something else to add to this discussion so why don't you tell me what it is."

Edward looked at Mac with a knowing grin and said, "One of the other things that is mentioned in a number of those sci-fi books is the movement of objects by means of magnetic brain waves sometimes called telepathy. One of the books from the mid-twenty-first century uses this telepathic method to move very large objects and it got me thinking. Could we not find a way where this might work on a starship?"

Mac was totally flabbergasted as she stared at Edward and said, "We do not have the ability to telepathically connect to this starship and tell it to move to distant locations instantly!"

"That's true, Mac. But we might just have the scientific equivalent to it," stated Edward.

"And what might that be?" asked Mac.

"Computers!" exclaimed Edward Butler.

"What in this galaxy are you talking about!?" But even as she said it, an idea was forming in her brain. She hesitated and then said. "Wait a minute! If I understand you correctly, you're talking about a possible interface of the ship's main computer with, what, the navigational computer and/or the transport computer? But they already communicate with each other anyway."

"I know," said Edward. "But they don't all do so simultaneously. Besides, Chief Davis told me that the interface with the transport computer was limited to only the actual transporting event. He said that the pre-transport coordinates were solely the task of that computer alone. He was the designer and engineer of that program and he felt that the only connection and backup to the main computer should be during the transport itself. I am suggesting that we reprogram the system to include the three previously mentioned systems incorporating the new high-speed transport capabilities."

"We will have to enlist the aid of both Chief Stokley 'Stokes' and Lindsey Thompson since the chief designed and engineered the transport computer and Lindsey, as our chief tech, was instrumental in helping me to figure out Ansmed's ability to transport undetected from the *Hawk* and it was her expertise that allowed us to improve on it." As Mac said this, she realized that she had bought into Edward's idea and wanted to move forward with it.

Little did they know how important this experiment would prove to be.

After Grannison and ND boarded the *Armstrong* shuttle and flew down to the surface of Janos, Keanyn turned to Cheng and asked her how things were working out with Salfrod working for her on the shuttle deck. She responded, "Very nicely, captain. He's one of the hardest workers I have." She then looked straight at Keanyn and with a suspicious grin said, "Remember, sir, I know you pretty well and I can sense another reason for your question other than an interest in how well Salfrod is doing."

"Drat!" exclaimed the Captain. "I thought that sounded like a perfectly casual question. Did my face give me away?"

Cheng returned with, "Nothing about your voice or facial expression tipped me off, sir. It's just that my whole experience serving with you all these years now has made me so familiar with your methods. Besides, take into consideration that my duties in my family's 'business' consisted of being a lookout and sizing up the individuals we came in contact with. Add to that the fact that I had been doing that since I was six years old and I think you see how easy it is for me to know where you're coming from."

Robert Porter, who had stayed with the other two on the shuttle deck, spoke up. "Uh oh! Captain, we're all going to have to be a lot more careful about what we say around the lieutenant here. I mean, it's going to be impossible to ever give her a surprise party!"

Cheng shot a look at Robert and stated, "Commander Porter, sir, I can turn off my deep observation abilities at any time and frequently do so. For instance, I chose to ignore whether your comment contained any other motive than the simple warning you gave to the captain."

Robert said, "She's good, captain. She's very good!"

Keanyn replied, "Oh, she's certainly that, commander, but I think we're skating on thin ice with her right now and I do need her assistance for something. Therefore, my dear Cheng, I apologize for both Robert and I and would like to ask for your know-how on a project I have in mind."

"Of course, sir," came her reply. "I would be happy to help you with any project."

Keanyn held up his hand as if to say, "just a minute." "This is a project that is part of our work as an investigative team so there is no need for using rank protocol. First names only, please."

Both Robert and Cheng nodded their heads in agreement. Then Cheng said, "So, what is this project you have in mind, Keanyn, and how does it involve Salfrod?"

"Once again, Cheng, very astute of you," remarked Keanyn with a look of approval. "My idea does indeed focus on the use of Salfrod so, subsequently, I must ask you another question concerning him. How far do you think we can trust him?"

Cheng's reply was swift and certain. "I would trust him to the limit, Keanyn." When she received looks of surprise from both men she added, "I have been observing him from the first minute I came in contact with him and I recognized, immediately, his sincerity when he declared his disdain for the purpose of the mission he had become a part of once he realized it's full extent. Now that I have had the opportunity to interact with him day to day, I have no doubt that he has become a full supporter of our mission."

"Your trust in him is extremely important in what I am about to suggest," declared Keanyn. "I propose to use Salfrod to lure Ansmed onto this ship in an effort to neutralize him and his ship once and for all. First, though, we need the intel ND, Stenn, and General Beckton can give us from Janos."

"In what capacity do you plan to use Salfrod?" queried Cheng.

Keanyn replied with, "I would like to send Salfrod down to Janos by setting up a ruse that he had gained our trust by appearing to become sympathetic to our cause, getting assigned to the shuttle deck, and then stealing a shuttle to escape to Janos to make his way to the Saffo V embassy in order to find Ansmed or get word to him that he has important information that will help him reach his purpose."

"How do you propose to make this ruse look authentic?" wondered Cheng.

Keanyn outlined his plan. "We are going to rely heavily on the rumor mill in order to convince certain people that Salfrod had indeed put one over on us."

"I think I'm following you, Keanyn," said Cheng.

Robert also nodded his head as if he had picked up on Keanyn's plan as well. He put his thoughts into words and said, "You want to make sure that the mole Ansmed has installed on the ship will be convinced that Salfrod is still on their side and, thus, won't be tipped off to our plan."

"Since, I assume, the mole you are referring to is the same individual who met Salfrod on the shuttle when he transported from the *Hawk* and gave him that nasty cosh on his head, that's the main one," stated the captain. "But since a lot of activity has occurred in the meantime, I would not be surprised if there weren't one or two more on board."

Robert was smiling ruefully as he agreed with Keanyn's thought, "I have no doubt that you are correct, Keanyn. In fact, we have tracked at least five individuals who transported onto the *Mall* starship as highly suspicious in just the last two ports of call."

Keanyn was a bit shaken by this revelation as he worriedly spoke, "That's a bit more alarming than I had even imagined, Robert. Have you been able to keep them under surveillance or determine their intent for being here?"

"Not to worry," assured Robert. "Two of them proved to be here for unrelated and rather petty issues that we resolved quite quickly. Two of the other three were somewhat more serious. They may have been tied to Ansmed's ship. We kept a tight surveillance on them, one of which was a female," said the head of security. "She was an Andromedian from Caltha, the fourth planet in the Andromeda system."

"What I am about to reveal to you is something I've only just now, in the last twelve hours, been able to prove conclusively," stated Robert. "While the Andromedian and her secretary obtained the deadly information that brought about the collapse of the A deck walls, they were not the ones who carried it out."

A puzzled Keanyn asked, "How did they accomplish that without being detected?"

Robert said, "That is explained when you understand the nature and talents of Andromedians."

"Aren't they the original inhabitants of that system who developed a method of mind reading?" asked Cheng with keen interest.

Robert replied, "Yes they are, Cheng, and that is why we paid particular attention to her. It's known that Andromedians rarely travel outside their own solar system and when they do, it's either for diplomatic or mysterious purposes. She appeared to be on a minor diplomatic mission to meet with Mrs. Pickle concerning setting up retail establishments on her home planet. The second individual posed as her secretary."

Cheng finished the explanation, "We are not stopping in the Andromeda system this time and she came here because of that to discuss their desire to establish a consumer retail system. Am I right?"

"On the surface, yes, Cheng," said Robert, "but that was only a cover. We discovered that she was also interested in how the A deck operated. She was quite transparent about it and didn't seem to have an ulterior motive, but we were on high alert just the same."

Keanyn now asked with a good deal of concern, "Why wasn't the investigative team apprised of this development, Robert, and how could a diplomatic mission, however minor, take place without my being informed of it?"

"I'm sorry," said Robert. "But protocol does not call for any officials from the ship's command to be informed of any minor diplomatic visits that deal solely with the shopping mall. Doing so at that time may have alerted the Andromedian to our suspicions so I refrained from informing you until we had solid proof of her true intentions. They left without giving any such proof. Or so we thought!" When he finished, Robert had a look of shame. He followed that with a statement, "I can't tell you how shocked I was when I learned this morning about the activity of those two Andromedians."

Keanyn addressed Robert saying, "I know you feel responsible for not finding this out sooner and, possibly, preventing the sabotage. But, my friend, we were all looking in so many places and watching so many people that our chances of thwarting the sabotage were very slim. I am curious, though. How did you discover that those Andromedians obtained the A deck information and passed it on to the ones who used it for the sabotage?"

Robert answered, "I was talking to Ross two days ago. I asked him if he was able to keep Mrs. Pickle from going completely overboard in her promotion of the mall. He answered by saying that she had been able to keep herself in check for the most part except for one or two instances. The first one he related dealt with her taking a small group of dignitaries to her observation platform and gushing profusely about her wonderful accomplishment. The second one caused him some concern until he questioned her closely."

"It involved her taking a diplomat and her secretary on a tour of the A deck and its control room. When he pressed her about what those two did while they were in the control room, she said that it wasn't much more than casually looking around and noting that such a complex function as the A deck could be controlled from such a small room and they left. They had only been in the room for less than five minutes."

"Were you still concerned, Robert?" asked Cheng.

"Yes!" Was his definite reply. "In fact, I went to the crewman who had been manning the A deck control room at the time to get his take on the situation. His answer matched that of Mrs. Pickle and I felt no longer concerned.

"But, this morning, my curiosity concerning Anromedians caused me to read up on them, and that's when I learned of their ability to project erroneous thoughts into the minds of others. That made me very suspicious and, when I questioned Mrs. Pickle if she had noticed any time discrepancies about that incident, she said that later that day it appeared as if she had lost nearly an hour of time. When I asked the crewman the same, he said that his relief had come to replace him earlier than he had expected, but he said it was easy to lose track of time when working in the control room."

Keanyn concluded, "So you immediately suspected that the Andromedian and her secretary had actually spent nearly an hour in the control room and used that time to learn about the fail-safe and familiarize themselves with the A deck controls so they could sell that information to the highest bidder."

"And that highest bidder proved to be Ansmed," remarked Cheng.

"Also they had closely examined the control door mechanism and figured out how to jam it," said Robert, and added, "And I believe that it was Ansmed who sent them to our ship, knowing of their skill and paying them handsomely to use it."

"That explains a lot," stated Keanyn. "And it suggests that we need to talk to Mrs. Pickle and see what other information she can give us that might prove to be useful."

"Might it also be advisable to have Suffaw with us when we do so?" asked Robert. "It seems that when you get the two of them together, their 'conversations' usually elicit a fair amount of information. I mean, they each know how to push the other's buttons."

Keanyn looked a little doubtful but, finally, said, "If we are very careful so as to not give anything away about our investigations, especially Suffaw's involvement in them, then I think we could use him as a catalyst to get her talking."

Cheng focused her attention on Robert and said, "You mentioned one other who had transported onto this ship who caused you concern, Robert. Who was that and how did things turn out with them?"

Robert shot a keen glance Cheng's way and explained, "It was a human who spent an inordinate amount of time in what appeared to be undercover visits to engineering. We wanted to observe him until we could get a clear idea of his intent. Then, one day, one of the techs assisting 'Stokes' on the retro engine's computer noticed him and confronted him. When the chief came on the scene, he grabbed hold of the skulker and gave him a hug and slap on the back. The two of them started laughing and throwing air punches at each other. Turns out, it was the chief's nephew who was trying to play a trick on Stokes by coming unannounced to the *Mall* starship. He had made a harmless tweak to the retro computers that made it appear that the engines had a possible malfunction just to prove to his uncle that he could do it. I understand he got a good talking to by his uncle and an assignment to clean out the vent traps in the latrines in the Raushdonian pub."

The other two immediately covered their mouths as if they were about to vomit. Keanyn spoke in a tone of pure disgust saying, "That is the one place where every species on board this ship uses the head. I had the great displeasure of being a recipient of the odor coming from those vents when I was asked if I would inspect them soon after the ship launched." He was nearly gagging from the memory.

"Who in the galaxy asked you to do that?" asked Cheng with a look of nausea.

"Suffaw's cousin who runs the pub—and who was prompted by him to do so, as I later learned," said Keanyn in reply.

Robert commented by stating, "Apparently you hadn't had much exposure to Raushdonians before that little incident. Oh well, live and learn."

Keanyn spoke, bringing their thoughts back to the saboteurs, "With all that you've told us, Robert, there's all the more reason to get Ansmed on this ship. It might flush his accomplice out and we can take care of both of them at one time."

Cheng voiced her thoughts, "And here I thought I might squeeze in some nap time, but that's not going to happen now. Oh, well! Never a dull moment aboard the *Mall* starship!"

THE CROCKETT

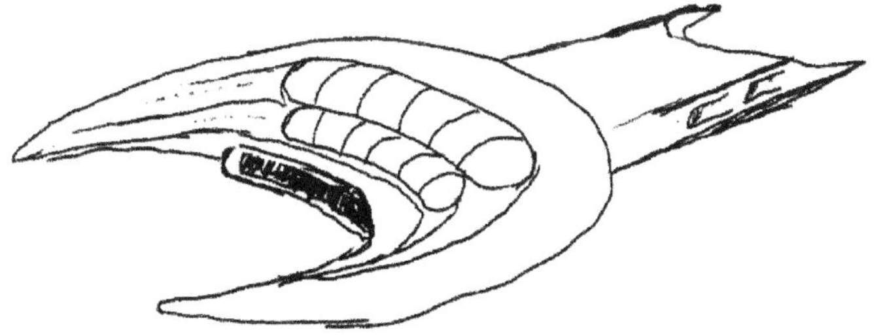

CHAPTER EIGHT

ON JANOS

The shuttle deck was beginning to get busy as several of the shuttles were being prepped to go down to Janos. Permission had finally been given for the crew of the starship to go down to the planet for some much-needed R & R as long as the groups numbered no more than five including a Legion assigned supervisor to make sure no questionable behavior occurred. While the crew was a bit offended by what they considered baby-sitting, Commander Dek of the IA division's Legion-assigned investigation team was still suspicious of the *Mall* starship's involvement in its own sabotage and wasn't willing to give officers and crew of the ship free reign to go or do whatever they wanted. Just another minor obstacle they had to work around.

At this rush of activity, Cheng spoke, "I believe our little conversation will have to come to an end, captain. I am going to be busy for the next hour or so."

"By all means, lieutenant," said Keanyn. "In fact, we all need to tend to duties. Robert, I assume you are planning to monitor ND's progress on Janos?"

Robert firmly nodded his head as he added, "That and give her any information we can dig up as to Stenn's exact location in the Saffo V embassy. I've already established a link with General Beckton's group which has proven to be helpful."

"Good," said Keanyn, "I will keep in touch with both of you so that we can coordinate our movements going forward. So now, let's get on with it!"

***

Stenn was trying to make himself invisible as he stood behind a giant potted plant of a rather strange alien origin in the reception area of the Saffo V embassy on the planet Janos. He had been in the embassy for four days now and had posed as a waiter, chauffeur, and messenger for the diplomatic staff. It was in this last capacity that he had picked up some valuable information concerning the whereabouts and status of Ambassador Calluran. It was now clear that the ambassador was here under duress and not willingly. He was being kept comfortably enough in one of the state guest rooms but would only leave the room under the watchful eyes of two guards posing as security for him.

Stenn was now incognito in the reception area because, in total confusion to him, his mother was there on some kind of diplomatic mission that he knew had to be completely bogus. His confusion didn't stem from the obvious pseudo-diplomacy that his mother was carrying out, but from the fact that she was interfering with his undercover mission. She rarely poked her nose in the middle of one of his assignments unless she needed to get a message to him and there was no other way of doing so, or if he was in need of her protection in some way he was unaware of.

"I understand that you, Assistant Ambassador Dunford, are here to request an audience for your head ambassador, aah," the embassy's chief secretary, Radule Omnivie, momentarily hesitated as he checked his records for the name of the head ambassador from Earth's International Agricultural Alliance and couldn't find it. He said apologetically, "I don't seem to have that information just at hand right now, Madam Dunford. I'm certain the office has sent up the wrong papers. I will see to this oversight immediately!" There was a fine sheen of a greenish-blue liquid glazing his forehead. This is what passed as perspiration on the skin of the slightly reptilian race of Lazarecs, an indigenous humanoid people who made up about 35 percent of the population of Saffo V.

ND, posing as the assistant ambassador of the fictitious Agricultural Alliance, had basically bullied her way into the meeting with the chief secretary and was not about to panic at the possibility of discovery when it was found that neither the agency, let alone an ambassador, even existed. She just continued to push ahead aggressively, as was her style.

"Chief secretary, I have not come here to twiddle my thumbs waiting for you to chastise an underling for their ineptitude in order for you to save face as we say on earth. I will bypass your lack of preparedness if we can get on with my preliminary tour of your facilities!"

ND had learned early on that, other than the top echelon, bureaucrats were easily intimidated and often failed to double-check their records to verify the authenticity of anyone claiming to be an official representative when so intimidated.

Therefore, she had no fear that her credentials would

be closely scrutinized and found to be false. Her entry into the embassy was facilitated by a very official-looking document (which she kept on hand for just such occasions) signed by Captain Keanyn Mathews. When the embassy communicated with the captain of the *Mall* starship and received his enthusiastic backing of Madam Dunford, there was no need to check any further.

With no need to involve security, Radule welcomed the diplomat with open arms.

"I would be most happy to give you the tour myself, Madam Dunford," said the secretary fawningly.

"I am flattered that such an important person as yourself would make such an offer, but I am certain that I would be keeping you from much more vital duties," stated ND. She knew that, after being intimidated, officials became even more cooperative when cajoled. This did not fail to work on the chief secretary.

"Well, I have to admit that I do have some very important papers to look over and it does need to be done, how do you say it on Earth, AP?" declared Radule.

"I think you mean ASAP, sir," noted N D with a smile. She continued to butter up the Lazerec secretary. "Of course, Mr. Secretary. It's only natural that someone in your position would have such pressing issues at hand. Perhaps you might have a page available or even a temporary member of staff from Earth that could perform the tour? For instance, what about that fellow over there by that beautiful potted plant?"

She pointed directly at Stenn, who shuffled away from the vegetation with his head slightly down to denote his subservient position.

Good, she thought. *He's playing the role nicely. Humble, but not exaggerating it.*

Radule Omnivie motioned for a junior staffer to bring Stenn over to them. When he was in front of them, the secretary asked him, "What are your duties here and when were you assigned to the embassy?"

Stenn raised his head a fraction and spoke softly but clearly. "I asked for an assignment to your embassy because I'm interested in the diplomatic corps. I have been serving in security on the *Mall* ship under Lieutenant Commander Porter, head of security, and he approved of my temporary assignment here. I've only been here a few days, but I have become quite familiar with the embassy due to my being used as a messenger for the staff."

"I see," said the Lazerec. "And what is your name?"

"Dominic Faldono, sir," answered Stenn. This had been the agreed-upon name Stenn would use if he was confronted by someone at the embassy. That name, coupled with the mention of Robert as his superior, would guarantee that, when it was checked out, his identity would be confirmed.

"I will contact your ship to verify your statement, Mr. Faldono," said Radule authoritatively. "Just a formality, you understand, but necessary." Stenn nodded his head in acknowledgment.

In a matter of one minute, the verification was made and Stenn was commissioned to guide his mother, as Madam Dunford, on a tour of the Saffo V embassy.

"A diplomat representing the International Agricultural Alliance!?" asked Stenn with incredulity. "And Madam Dunford! What hat did you draw that name out of?"

They were walking down a corridor toward the embassy's dining hall where they would most likely find solitude at the time of 16:70 drolmunds. This time was equivalent to 2:30 p.m. on Earth. Right between lunch and dinner.

They entered the dining hall before she could answer

and took two seats around a small table in a corner of the room.

"We had very little time to come up with anything more plausible than that," asserted his mother.

"And what's more," she added, "we needed to act before you put a plan into action. Keanyn has come up with a way to get Ansmed on the *Mall* ship in order to trap him there and pull the plug on any further damage he might be planning. We also need to find out if you've learned anything about Ambassador Calluran and work that into our plan."

Stenn adjusted himself in his chair so that he could see out the small window tucked into the alcove where they were sitting. He sounded a bit disappointed and said, "I was on my way to contact General Beckton when I looked into the reception hall and saw you standing there as clear as daylight. I was wondering what in the galaxy had brought you there and hoped it wasn't to abort my mission when I heard you present yourself as some under secretary of a fictitious agency. Then you pointed right at me and I thought you had gone out of your mind."

His mother chuckled as Stenn described the scene from his viewpoint. She looked at her son with a tender smile and stated, "I'll admit, I was flying by the seat of my pants just then, but when I saw you I knew it was a golden opportunity to save a lot of time looking for you so that we could team up and help bring Keanyn's plan to fruition."

Stenn then emphatically stated, "You know, Mother, that captain of ours could have a wonderful future in security and espionage if he wasn't wasting it on commanding the starship. What all is included in this plan of his?"

"He's thought of a way to lure Ansmed to the ship in order to flush out his accomplice or accomplices," ND began. She then detailed Salfrod's involvement in the scheme and more about her mission on the planet. Her next question was key, "Have you been able to determine the status of Ambassador Calluran?"

"I most certainly have!" exclaimed Stenn. "You'll be glad to know that it appears that the ambassador is here, more or less, as a prisoner and doesn't appear to have had anything to do with the insidious plot of his nephew. It seems that Ansmed initially used his uncle's contacts and influence to equip his ship with state-of-the-art computers, technicians, and transport software. Which, we now know they developed into a faster undetectable form of transport. Then he brought in engineers from the Legion's elite engineering school to develop and equip his ship with the new XT1 power thruster engines."

ND was thunderstruck as she said, "My word! Stenn, it's as if he were preparing his ship for war!"

"That he was, Mother, that he was," confirmed her son. "What's more, he was also making it look like his uncle was approving of his plan by getting him to sign for a few minor improvements to the *Hawk* then taking his signature off those documents and transferring them to the documents for the more high-tech and deadly equipment. With the busy schedule of the ambassador and his naive trust in his nephew's claim to be on the side of the Earth's contribution, he never suspected Ansmed's involvement in any clandestine activity."

"But surely he wasn't as blind as all that! He must have figured something out at some point!" stated ND in an exasperated tone.

Stenn gently grabbed his mother's right hand and gave it a reassuring squeeze. He knew that, as much as she worked hard not to show any kinks in her emotional armor, she was fond of Ambassador Calluran and never wanted to truly believe he had been involved in the sabotage plot. He said, "Of course he didn't remain clueless. Do you remember when it was reported to our team that the ambassador was overheard saying something about being disrespected by a family member?"

"Yes," said ND. "I think it was Edward who overheard the ambassador's enigmatic comment."

Stenn nodded his head saying, "That's right! I have discovered that the ambassador had just received news about Ansmed's activities and was on his way to confront him. That confrontation led to Ambassador Calluran's kidnapping during the sabotage of the A deck."

"How do you know this?" questioned his mother.

"Easy," said Stenn. "I've found the ambassador and have had a chance to communicate with him."

Grannison Loche was having a drink with General Beckton in the general's office. They were discussing Stenn's predicament and his mother's attempt to find out what was going on and help him. Grannison was asking the general a question as he held up his glass of one of the finest single malt scotches he had ever tasted and looked intently at its beautiful clearness swishing around in its container.

"Why did you wait so long to contact the starship, sir? Wasn't four days a bit much?"

"Believe me, commander, if it had been my way, I would have contacted you the minute Stenn entered the embassy. But he insisted I give him three days to dig up something before letting his colleagues know he was in there. He said that three days would be all he needed to uncover what was going on and he could present the mission as a done deal," said Beckton in a rueful manner.

The general continued his explanation, "When he failed to get back here in the three days, I gave him one more night. But by this morning, I couldn't wait any longer. I just hope ND doesn't get herself trapped in there as well."

"I've gotten to know those two pretty well, general, and I'm sure that, between the two of them, they'll get to the bottom of what's going on in that embassy," stated Grannison affirmatively. "Captain Mathews and Lieutenant Porter have concocted a pretty good plan for getting the information we need and getting them out safely."

General Beckton stood up and his six-foot, three-inch frame topped with a full head of dark brown wavy hair and well-groomed beard and mustache was poised in casual attention. He looked directly at Grannison and said, "Commander Loche, I have known Captain Mathews for quite some time, as you well know, and any plan that hatches from that brain will be sufficiently devious enough to succeed."

Just then, a quiet knock consisting of two short and three long taps came from the rear entrance of the general's office. This had been the agreed-upon signal that Stenn was at the door. Beckton walked over and gave three quick staccato-like knocks with the response being one quick knock in return.

The general let Stenn and his mother in and they sat down on two of the four upholstered leather armchairs that faced General Beckton's impressive desk. Well, to be truthful, this was actually the ambassador's office in the Earth's embassy on Janos. The ambassador, Sir Rodney Finchem, had graciously appointed the general acting ambassador while he made a diplomatic visit to Janos's sister planet, Renos.

After accepting two glasses of scotch, ND started the

conversation. "It's been a while since I've been out in the field on a mission," she said with some excitement. "I must admit that I've missed it. I think I'll start doing a little more of it. Can't let Stenn have all the fun." As she finished, she had the wry smile she often made when she was pleased with herself or poking fun.

Stenn came back with, "Actually, Mother, I thought you were missing some of your polished quickness out there. A little rusty, perhaps?"

"Apparently the mission was successful," stated Grannison with a chuckle.

While the general could appreciate the lighthearted mood of mother and son, he was anxious to hear the results of their endeavors. He brought the festivities to a more serious mood.

"All kidding aside, what did you find out was going on in that embassy? Since you were in there for four days, why don't you speak first, Stenn."

"We did more than find out what was going on, general. We got the wheels rolling to get Ambassador Calluran safely out of the embassy because he is not a conspirator in the plot of his nephew Ansmed but is, instead, a prisoner," stated Stenn with assurance. "Once I located him on my second day there, I managed to get a message to him as a runner for the head of staff. I had already ascertained that he was not there of his free will. Even though he had not been forcibly detained, they kept him under heavy guard and never let him roam about freely." Now Stenn got more serious saying, "He informed me of a plot by Ansmed that contains subtleties I would not have expected from Ansmed. If they prove successful, they will erode the confidence in our mission that we worked so hard to obtain and could prove to be the straw that broke the camel's back."

On the *Mall* starship, Salfrod was about to board the small shuttle, *Grissom*, when a message arrived for Cheng from General Beckton on Janos. He had gone directly to Cheng, bypassing the captain, because Grannison had informed him that the plan to spring Salfrod from the ship down to the planet was due to begin in just a matter of minutes and there was no time to lose.

"Has Salfrod left yet, Cheng?" shouted the general by means of a coded comm link. "We have very important information to give you that will affect his mission!"

Cheng reacted quickly to the message and grabbed the comm mic, switching it to direct contact with the shuttle. She excitedly spoke into the mic, "Salfrod, delay commencement of the mission. Vital info is coming from Janos!" She, then, switched the comm to the shuttle bay so that all those involved in the false escape plan would be aware of the change. "I need you all to stand down for a few minutes while we implement some new information into our plan."

She turned back to communicating with the general, and said, "General Beckton, what is this new information? I certainly hope we can incorporate it quickly. Our plan is based on split-second timing."

"This info will affect how you handle the ambassador's situation," said Beckton. "We are now certain that he is a prisoner and not a conspirator. Therefore, Salfrod will have to convince Ansmed to use him as a bargaining chip."

Grannison broke in, "Cheng, is Keanyn getting this link, now?"

Cheng answered, "I've patched this communication into the captain's personal unit and he's getting everything."

"Good," said Grannison. "I've told the general about Keanyn's plan to lure Ansmed onto the *Mall* ship. Salfrod will still tell Ansmed about his apparent change of heart concerning the Earth's mission so that he could obtain vital information, escape from the ship, and make his way to Ansmed. The new twist is telling Ansmed that he believes the command staff on the ship knows who his accomplice on board is. Salfrod will then act as a conduit between Ansmed and his accomplice. But, in actuality, he will feed that one false information to confuse any further plans of Ansmed. Salfrod is then going to attempt to encourage Ansmed to transport to the *Mall* ship and silence the accomplice. He is certain that only Ansmed knows the identity of that accomplice and won't want to reveal it to anyone else for security purposes."

"Is Ansmed in the embassy, Grann?" Keanyn asked. He had heard most of the conversation and wanted to get down to the nitty-gritty. "Salfrod must get word directly to him for our plan to work. Especially by using Ambassador Calluran as a bargaining chip?"

Stenn broke into the conversation saying, "Keanyn, this is Stenn. My mother and I have gotten out of the embassy with this information. I've spoken to the ambassador briefly and can confirm his status there. I'm confident that if Salfrod can convince Ansmed to bring his uncle with him to the ship in order to use him to bargain for a trade for the accomplice, we can snatch Ansmed and the accomplice and put them under arrest for murder and treasonous activity against the Legion."

ND spoke up with a cautionary comment, "If we don't capture Ansmed, Keanyn, the blood bath he is sure to bring will make anything so far pale by comparison. As for Ansmed's whereabouts, he moves regularly between his ship and the embassy. His ship is docked on the dark side of Janos's third moon, Pasqua."

Robert Porter, who had been summoned by Keanyn to join him on his way to the shuttle deck chimed in, "You two have done some great work down there, ND, but I'm a bit anxious about your comment about Ansmed's plan. Just what has he got up his sleeve?"

"He won't be satisfied even if his subtle plans are successful. In the end he wants nothing less than a wholesale massacre of the entire *Mall* fleet and anyone who comes to our aid!" exclaimed Stenn with panic in his voice.

Keanyn spoke with some confusion, "I know that we only have Dooley's ship, the *Gator*, with full weapons capabilities, but the Janovian fleet of Legion ships should come to our assistance. That's far too much firepower for the *Hawk* to go up against and succeed."

"You may be underestimating the attack capabilities of Ansmed's ship, Keanyn," ND interjected. "Besides, he may not be interested in winning a battle as long as he can destroy Earth's contribution."

"In any case," stated Robert. "How do we proceed with our plan for Salfrod? Do you think he's capable of adapting to this new info on the fly, Cheng?"

"Ask him yourself, Robert. I've had him connected to this entire conversation," remarked the shuttle deck commander.

"How very aware of you, lieutenant," stated the head of security sarcastically. He addressed Salfrod. "What do you think, Salfrod? Can you adapt your conversation with Ansmed to reflect this new info and convince him to follow your direction?"

The former stowaway spoke confidently into his comm unit, "Lieutenant Commander Porter, I had fairly close dealings with Ansmed before being transported to this ship. I saw how determined he is to thwart the mission of the *Mall* starship, though I wasn't aware to what villainous extent he was willing to take it. I also took note of his pride and witnessed how someone could use that to cause him to be influenced to act according to their wishes. I'm certain I can accomplish the same especially if he is impressed with my escape from this ship with such vital information."

"Well," said Keanyn. "It's time to get this show on the road. "Cheng, get the rest of your people up to speed with our altered plan quickly. Grannison, how soon can you get off the planet and back up here with Stenn and ND?"

Grannison answered with a look in ND's direction. "I think we'll have to go back to the embassy in order to cover our tracks. If we just leave the planet without some formal reason for our withdrawal, it will arouse a good bit of suspicion from the chief secretary who would probably dig deeper than he previously did and discover Ambassador Dunford and her agency are a little less than genuine."

ND finished the statement by saying, "That would definitely get back to Ansmed and put him on the alert and put Salfrod in a very precarious position."

"Take care of that as quickly and efficiently as you can," Keanyn told them. "We won't be able to launch Salfrod out of here until you extricate yourselves from there properly."

"Roger that, captain," barked out Grannison.

Keanyn looked anxious and said, "I have every confidence in you, commander."

Commander Loche stated, "We shouldn't be any longer than an hour unless we run into complications at the embassy. ND and Stenn nodded their heads in agreement so we'll see you in an hour."

It took them exactly fifty-six minutes and twenty-two seconds to get to the embassy, tell Secretary Omnivie that ND along with her guide, Dominic, had been called back to the ship to host a last-minute reception dinner. Keanyn had also informed them that Cheng had put some more of her former skills to work in arranging for several diplomats and embassy officials to back up the status of ND's fictitious under-secretary position in the bogus cabinet office in order to convince Ansmed in case he got wind of Madam Dunford's visit. This made her and Stenn's departure from the planet less worrisome. Therefore, they boarded the *Grissom*, and flew up to the *Mall* ship confident that their ruse would not be discovered too soon.

"Good to see the three of you back," declared Keanyn with a broad smile. He turned to ND's son and said, "Especially you, Stenn. We have all been very anxious about your safety since you entered the embassy. As usual, though, you have come away with valuable information." The captain shook Stenn's hand firmly while putting an arm around him and slapping his back.

Robert added to the greeting, saying, "Even I was a little worried. Of all the missions Stenn has been on, this one was the most important as far as the potential intelligence was concerned and the most dangerous both to our mission and his safety. I should have known he would succeed in spades. Now we can start our little play acting with Salfrod."

"And not a moment too soon!" noted Cheng. While she was glad for the return of the three, there was frustration in her voice over the delay in starting Salfrod's staged escape. She continued into the comm mic, "Salfrod, I hope you've brushed up on your acting skills. You'll need them!"

The Cherillian answered, "I won't need to alter my story too much. And, after all, conning someone isn't so much about what you say but how you say it."

"I guess those lessons with Saffaw paid off," said Keanyn. "It seems like the schooling in 'con artistry 101' that Saffaw taught Salfrod is about to come to fruition."

Robert Porter commented, "Saffaw did say that Salfrod was a willing student who was quick to learn."

"He'll have to be if he is to convince Ansmed to come aboard this ship," noted Stenn, as he took his small stun blaster out of its hidden compartment below the right front pocket on his trousers. "It feels good to get that thing out of its holster. It may be small, but it rubs a bruise on my lower thigh after I wear it so long and I've had it on for four days."

Cheng addressed her crew of pilots and shuttle bay personnel over the comm unit, "Is everyone ready to launch this escape and battle play? We must make it look real folks. This new info doesn't affect our little deception. So I'm confident in our success." She put two thumbs up as she stood on the balcony-like upper level that gave an open view of the deck floor below. All those on the deck floor returned her thumbs up with ones of their own.

When the order was given to commence operations, Salfrod powered up and quickly blasted out from the shuttle deck as if being pursued by the entire fleet of Legion warships. Thirty seconds later, a small group of shuttle fighter craft emerged from the ship intent on tracking the thief down and blasting him out of existence.

At first, it appeared that the purloined shuttle was evading the oncoming fighters, but a well-aimed laze-beam shot from one of the pursuers appeared to hit Salfrod's ship just aft of its starboard fuel cell. This caused the *Grissom* to yaw to the left and begin a roll that Salfrod managed to control. Of course, this was all part of the choreographed display to convince the Saffo V embassy—and particularly Ansmed—that Salfrod had made off with the shuttlecraft and it had been damaged in the process.

The *Grissom* did experience blast damage but it had been rigged to explode at a precise time and in a precise location on the shuttle so as to ensure no danger to the operation of the vessel. Several other shots flew by and one or two of them made glancing hits but no more were serious.

As Salfrod approached the landing pad at the Saffo V embassy, he radioed to the landing crew that he needed to see the highest official there as well as Ansmed due to the fact that he had vital information to relay to them.

Upon Salfrod's less-than-steady landing on the planet's surface, he was greeted by Chief Secretary Omnivie and a very suspicious-looking Ansmed, who immediately walked up to Salfrod as he emerged from the shuttle and said, "I hope you can give a good account of your actions here. It was my understanding that you had become a sympathetic member of their crew. I have already ordered the examination of the vid record of your escape from the *Mall* starship." As he noted the moniker of the Earth ship, a sneer and a disgusted look accompanied it.

"I would expect no less from you, Commander Kleek." Proclaimed Salfrod in, what he hoped was, a confident but subservient tone. Kleek was Ansmed's family name and commander was his self-appointed title. He continued, "I did indeed feign loyalty to their cause once I gained consciousness." He stopped and looked straight at Ansmed, speaking in a rather hurt tone. "Your plant on their ship and my liaison nearly killed me when I merely tried to sneak a peek at them. I'm certain that proved a setback to your plans since I was sent to the ship to get to the control room for the A deck and override its fail-safe mechanisms among other things."

Ansmed spoke with a continued hint of suspicion, "My operative on the Earth ship told me that you had refused to go forward with our plan when you discovered, because of their mistake of revealing too much of our plan to you, that we had told you everything you needed to know to accomplish your mission. There was no need for you to know that until you gained access to the control room. I admit that they became overzealous in their efforts to convince you otherwise, but we would have had to find an alternative to you in any case."

Salfrod had to think fast. "Of course, I did express some reluctance in carrying out my mission. After all, with not having been told the results of my manipulation with the fail-safes, it was a bit shocking to realize that there would be so much loss of life. By having that information kept from me, hearing it all of a sudden at such a critical moment made me reassess my involvement in the mission. If I had been completely informed beforehand, I could have either opted out or remained part of the plan. Then you wouldn't have lost precious time." As he finished, Salfrod knew he might have been a little too assertive but better to be chastised for that than accused of telling a pack of lies. Which may have happened anyway.

Ansmed was looking very closely at Salfrod, obviously deciding if he believed him. After nearly a minute, he said, "Either you're telling the truth or you're doing a great con job on me. I want to believe the latter but I don't remember you as being that clever. And as for taking such a bold stand like that in front of me, you would never have done that before. You've changed. You still haven't answered about if you were, or are, sympathetic to the ridiculous Earth project."

This was getting to be a tad more scrutinizing than Salfrod expected, but he calmed himself by taking a deep inner sigh before speaking, "The only reason the crew of the Earth ship believed that I was on their side was because I was very careful to give them that impression."

"Why do you think a statement like that is going to convince me that you weren't on their side?" declared the Doomrahnian.

"It won't," stated the Cherrilian. "You have to let me finish first, commander."

"Well, I beg your pardon, then," shot back Ansmed sarcastically. "Please, continue."

Salfrod smiled and proceeded, "Once I woke up from the terrible blow I received, I realized no one had noticed. So I decided to pretend that I was still unconscious and see what I could pick up from conversations around me. I learned that the success of their entire mission hung on the acceptance of each port of call to wholeheartedly endorse the *Mall* experience and report such to Legion headquarters. Small glitches could be tolerated and fixed. Major ones could, and probably would, spell doom."

"Did that influence you in any way?" asked Secretary Omnivie.

"I spent a considerable amount of time thinking about my loyalties and I realized that I still believed the Earth project to be completely inappropriate to the cause of the Galactic Legion. I now felt that the Legion itself had abandoned its purpose as well. If it was going to take a catastrophic event to derail Earth's project and bring the Legion back to its senses, then what you had planned, Commander Kleek, would have to go forward."

As Salfrod finished his statement, Ansmed and the Chief Secretary turned to look at each other. Ansmed made a flicking gesture with his head, and the two of them walked a few feet away to discuss the situation. After several minutes, during which Salfrod came close to panicking, they turned their attention back to the Cherrilian's story.

Commander Kleek began, "As I stated earlier, my tendency is to believe that we are being conned, except for two things. Your conduct and demeanor are so uncharacteristic but sincere, Salfrod. Secondly, Secretary Omnivie has reminded me that it was never reported that you actually said you had decided to join the Earth initiative. That was reported by my operative in the *Mall* as coming from some of the officers on the ship. They could have said that in order to throw us off, feeling as if we had another ally on board their ship." He paused before revealing their decision. He looked directly at Salfrod with sternness and said, "Therefore we have decided that you are, most likely, telling the truth and we can get some valuable information from you."

When Salfrod finally let out a noticeable sigh of relief, Ansmed warned him, "Don't think you are out of the woods yet, my friend. I intend to keep a close eye and a short leash on you. Everything you tell us will be double-checked. For instance, what do you know about my uncle, Ambassador Calluran?"

"Actually, that is the information I have that prompted me to plan my escape from the *Mall*!" stated Salfrod excitedly.

Both Ansmed and the secretary abruptly turned their heads and looked at each other with surprise and concern. It was Ansmed who turned back to address Salfrod. He was now very anxious to hear his report. "I am keenly interested in what you have to say. My uncle's involvement in this entire affair has been at the center of our plans."

Salfrod spoke knowing that what he was about to propose was vital to Keanyn and all the others on the investigative team.

"What I have to tell you will, I believe, require you to make some serious adjustments to your future plans. Therefore, may I suggest we go to a much more private location to discuss it, commander?"

Secretary Omnivie nodded his head in agreement as he addressed Commander Kleek. "I think that is very wise, Ansmed. As you know, our ambassador and his staff—including me—are behind you in your efforts to discredit and destroy the Earth's ridiculous contribution to the Legion. There are, however, a number of individuals at the embassy who are fully behind their frivolous and idiotic mission. Not to mention the majority of the inhabitants here on Janos. Therefore, a location out of earshot of such ones is desirable."

"You're absolutely right, Radule," said Ansmed. "In my excitement to hear Salfrod's information, I forgot where we were. I suggest we go to my offices in the embassy's annex. By the way, when is Ambassador Musslavo due back from his trip to Saffo V for the birth of his first grandchild?"

Secretary Radule Omnivie smiled warmly as he answered Ansmed's question. "Tomorrow, commander, and I'm certain he is going to want to be brought up to date on everything that's transpired since shortly after the sabotage on the *Mall* ship."

"He will certainly get three ears full, especially when we add what I hope will be the significant news Salfrod will disclose." As he said this, he threw a glance at the Cherillian as if to say, *and it better be good!*

They settled into Ansmed's office and the commander got straight to the point. "What have you got for us, Salfrod."

The Cherillian's wide nose flared as he took in a deep breath before beginning. "I became very conversant with the chief doctor, Alfred Karushkin, while on board the ship. He was kept abreast of some of the information being compiled by what they called the Sabotage Investigative Team, made up of most of the command staff. They were especially interested in finding out if Ambassador Calluran was a prisoner or ally of yours, Commander Kleek."

"How did they know that I had anything to do with my uncle's disappearance?" questioned Ansmed.

Salfrod knew he was asking to find out if he had something to do with giving that info to the *Mall's* officers. He answered truthfully. "I had no way of knowing your plans at that point, sir. In fact, it was reported to them by the staff of the Raushdonian pub in the mall that two Doomrhanians had escorted the ambassador into the pub after which he was never seen again on board the ship. They also knew that the two Doomrahnians were members of the crew of your ship, the *Hawk*."

Ansmed was taken aback by this revelation and he spoke with some concern. "I told those two to make sure they tried to keep their identities more difficult to identify. I should have paid the Andromedian females more and had them get my uncle off the *Mall* ship. Their skills at projecting and manipulating thoughts would have proven to be invaluable. But, that's 'water under the bridge,' as earthlings express it. I have also underestimated the thoroughness of the *Mall* command staff's detecting capabilities. That means they have looked into our transporting system. What have they learned about that?"

The answer Salfrod gave was a mixture of truth and falsehood. "Since my transfer to the ship was undetected, and would have remained so if I hadn't been coshed over the head and left to be found, they were immediately curious as to how I got there. They went over their vid records countless times and could only conclude that it was some new method of transporting and their technology was not up to par. This has been very frustrating to them as they can't prevent the transporting to or from your ship." Salfrod sensed that he had hooked his two listeners. "That brings me to the next crucial point. It was because they tried to figure out the transport issue, they found it came from the *Hawk*."

Ansmed was now truly worried. He had been counting on the high-tech transporting system and the anonymity of his involvement. He was beginning to think that his agent on board the *Mall* ship had become a major liability. If it wasn't for the action that the agent took against Salfrod, his plan would have moved along much more smoothly. He tabled that thought for now and focused back on the problem of the *Hawk* being identified. He addressed Salfrod. "Just how much do they know about my ship and me in particular?"

"A good deal, unfortunately," stated the Cherillian. Then he added, "Once they learned that I had transported over from the *Hawk*, it wasn't all that difficult to find out about you and how you had outfitted it with all the cutting-edge technology. Your relationship with Ambassador Calluran was already known, as well as how you had reclaimed your old ship with his help. They didn't know about the extent to which you had equipped it until recently, though."

"With what you've told us, we are going to have to step up our plans," noted Secretary Omnivie. We can't afford to wait for a force from the *Mall* ship's convoy to launch an attack on us and the embassy. We need to go on the offensive and soon!" He turned to Ansmed and said, "Do you concur with that, Commander Kleek?"

Ansmed looked sharply at the secretary and, with a furrowed brow and eyes squinted in annoyance, declared, "While I do feel we must accelerate the pace of our plans, Mr. Secretary, we don't need to react too swiftly to this information. We should have some time to make reasonably thought-out arrangements. How much time do you think we have, Salfrod?"

Salfrod couldn't believe how this conversation had taken a turn that could work very nicely with the suggestions he had been given to introduce. Therefore, with confidence, he started to direct their thoughts toward planning to go aboard the *Mall* starship. "Commander, any force from the convoy, not to mention any aid from the home forces on this planet, couldn't even begin to make an attack without the Earth officers presenting a proposal to the Legion and the Janovian Council while keeping it a secret from this embassy. Even with a rush put on the proceedings, it would take between a week to ten days, Earth time, to get approval, and another two days to implement it. That is the equivalent of two and three-fourths drolshuls in Saffo V time. And I must add, they are indeed forming a plan to attack the embassy and try to free your uncle, who they are fairly sure is being held against his will."

"My efforts to make it appear that my uncle was involved in the sabotage plot worked quite well for a good while," said Ansmed. "It kept probing eyes from looking too hard in my direction. I can also thank the embassy staff, especially Ambassador Musslavo and our good chief secretary here for their aid in deflecting any inquiries away from me." He performed a tip of an imaginary hat toward Radule.

The chief secretary returned a nod of appreciation toward Ansmed and commented, "The Ambassador and I share your disdain for the Earth's contribution, Ansmed, as you well know. We both believe that the Legion has gone off track from their initial purpose to build peace and unity among the member planets within the Legion's authority. We believe that goal can only be accomplished through strong central leadership and any planet's contribution should enhance that leadership."

Salfrod was momentarily stunned to hear such anarchist rhetoric pour from the mouth of Saffo V's chief secretary to the Janovian Embassy. *Great stars in the Galaxy!* he thought. *Is that what I signed on to support when I joined Ansmed's team?* Instead of showing any of these thoughts, he calmed himself and spoke. "I appreciate your viewpoint, chief secretary, but what are we going to do about the more immediate problem?"

Ansmed introduced his ideas, "We have a few options, I believe. One is to take my uncle out of here to a safe location, thus thwarting their plan to rescue him. Also, when we do that, we plant evidence that their belief he is a prisoner is wrong and that he is working as my partner. As such, he had been working undercover while on board the *Mall* ship and we took him off the ship to protect his imminent discovery.

"Two, we spring a swift but precise strike against the convoy. It is only protected by one heavily armed Battlestar cruiser, which the element of surprise will seriously impede. This latter option will tend to jeopardize our future effectiveness, but we can bide our time and recover. Do either of you have any other options?"

"I might have a third one," declared Salfrod. "Because I have a bit more information that might make it advisable to go this way."

The other two stared quizzically at Salfrod. Secretary Omnivie wondered how much information the Cherrilian had accumulated during his stay on the Earth ship. Ansmed wondered how much of that information he was not telling them.

"We're all ears. Unlike Radule, I have six listening orifices," declared Ansmed. "It takes a lot of info to fill them up."

Salfrod knew that Kleek was being facetious but he also detected a subtle threat in his tone. He outlined his option.

"I was saving this because I wanted to see if any of your ideas would make revealing it unnecessary." He shifted to a more comfortable position in his not-so-comfortable chair and continued, "I happened to overhear the captain and his chief of security, Robert Porter, discussing the possible identity of your operative on their ship, commander. They thought I had fallen unconscious after another round of their questioning me about trying to see if I could recall anything about my assailant. I honestly did have a mild case of amnesia and I never got a good look at your operative with the exception that I had the sense of a large female of alien origin."

"So you're telling me that you never saw my agent clearly enough to identify him or her?" asked Ansmed with some doubt.

Salfrod was a bit nervous as he knew his answer to Ansmed's question and subsequent statement were crucial in convincing the chief conspirator to buy into Keanyn's plan to lure him onto the *Mall* ship. Therefore, he chose his words carefully.

"Commander Kleek," he said. "I can assure you that what I told Captain Mathews and his security chief was all that I knew of the identity of your agent. Even then, it was barely a vague impression. What that little information did, though, was to get their team digging into the possibilities of who the sabotage agent as they called her—since I had given them the impression of a female—was."

"What were they able to come up with?" inquired Radule.

Salfrod had to be especially careful now. "Their job was not as difficult as you might think, sir. The number of alien races who are physically larger than humans is not all that numerous. About twenty-five to twenty-eight to choose from and only four are on board the *Mall* ship. They are the Meerdons from Pegasi b in the Pegasi star system, Sharlees from Iota Draconis b in the Draconion star system, the Larms from the Alluvian star system, and Gwalias from the very same star system in which we now find ourselves. They have narrowed it down to the Sharlees and the Meerdons."

"Of those four, I would think the Sharlees to be the least suspect," stated Radule somewhat surprised. "They are among the most jovial and fun-loving of races. When they get in trouble, it's usually for having pulled some prank, not interstellar terrorism or espionage."

At this point, Ansmed made an interesting comment, "People can get tired of always being thought of as harmless or not serious enough to make a difference in anything. I sometimes wonder if Sharlees act the fools in order to hide a darker side."

"Might that be because that's how you look at things? Through a darker lens?" noted Secretary Omnivie.

Ansmed answered, "I admit that I have a more cynical viewpoint than most, but there's good reason for that."

As he said this, there was a look of veiled sorrow on his face.

Salfrod, on the other hand, had zeroed in on Ansmed's

comment. He felt that the commander's words revealed that the Sharlees were involved with Commander Kleek's machinations. He now felt the time was right to bring up the plan.

"Gentlemen, with what we know, might a trip to the *Mall* ship to make an exchange be in order?"

Ansmed was fairly agitated by this question. He stepped closer to Salfrod looked straight at him and gestured emphatically as he said, "What do you mean by exchange? What do they have of value to us? I assume you are referring to my uncle as our bargaining chip. And why should we go to their ship for this exchange?"

Oh no, thought Salfrod. *I brought this up too soon. What did Robert teach me about turning a mistake into an advantage?* He looked straight back at Ansmed and firmly stated, "Why, commander, I would have thought the reasons would be perfectly clear. Take the initiative but not violently. By going to their ship to negotiate in peaceful terms, you throw them off guard. They may think that you have weakened in your resolve or feel that you can't succeed in destroying their mission."

Ansmed began to ponder Salfrod's line of reasoning, but it was Secretary Omnivie who spoke. "I do think that makes some sense, Commander Kleek. Giving them a false impression of our intentions would bring their guard down and make them more vulnerable to attack."

"There are some points to Salfrod's argument," noted Ansmed. "But just who are we exchanging my uncle for?"

Salfrod knew this would be the tricky part because Ansmed would be very reluctant to reveal the identity of his agent. So, he began by acknowledging that fact.

"I am aware of your desire to keep your operatives

anonymous, but, I'm afraid in this case, they will soon discover who the one on their ship is." He paused, then said ominously, "If they haven't already."

"You did say that they had narrowed it down to two races, correct?" asked Ansmed.

Salfrod responded, "Yes, the Meerdons and the Sharlees. Of those two, only the Sharlees have any females on board. But, remember, I couldn't be certain that it was a female who met me on the shuttle and gave me that love tap. It was, and still is, only an impression."

Radule speculated, "I still can't picture a Sharlee being involved in anything as clandestine or violent as what we have accomplished or are yet to do."

"Despite what our good secretary feels, you are suggesting we go aboard the Earth ship and bargain for a trade of my agent for my uncle? What if they haven't discovered the identity of my operative? That would make our visit there not only useless but dangerous!" exclaimed Ansmed forcefully.

Salfrod had expected this and was prepared with a contingency plan. He nodded his head in acknowledgment of Ansmed's reasoning and said, "That is a definite possibility, sir. Therefore I propose that we offer both your uncle and myself in exchange for your agent, whom you will transfer over to your ship without them learning their identity. You can say that their usefulness has lapsed but their implementation on future projects may be needed. That way, you protect their identity and they feel like they get the better of the deal, two for one."

Ansmed was still not sold completely. "What prevents them from identifying my agent once they discover who is missing?"

Salfrod had also accounted for this, saying, "If your

agent is a regular member of their crew, have them request a pass down to Janos for a few days of R&R before we arrive on the ship and then transfer someone else of that race to a remote Legion colony. By the time they get themselves back from there, our mission will have been accomplished. As for your true agent, you can use those few days of R&R to debrief, then re-brief them before sending them back. Now you have two agents on board the *Mall* ship, including myself."

"I must say, that sounds very plausible," said Secretary Omnivie with a bit of a smile on his face. A Lazarec's smile generally revealed two rows of smooth-edged, lightly green teeth on the bottom along with a very full upper lip and a slightly forked tongue. All of these features were visible on Radule Omnivie's visage.

"As to the plausibility of your suggestion, Salfrod, I believe there is a lot of risk involved. But the outcome may be worth it," stated Ansmed as he, finally, seemed to be buying Salfrod's plan.

CHAPTER NINE

MORE STRATEGIES

On the bridge of the *Mall* ship, Keanyn, Mac, Grannison and the rest of the bridge crew assigned at that particular time were merely manning their stations as they had been for the past thirty-two days in lockdown.

"Have you heard the latest accusation Commander Dek has leveled against us?" questioned JA from his seat in the communication pod.

Grannison rose from his seat, walked over to stand by JA, and leaned against the railing that formed a boundary around the comm officer's station. He proceeded to address the bridge in imitation of the IA's chief investigator.

"It has come to my attention, gentlemen, that you permitted a certain shuttle, commandeered by a treasonous stowaway, to escape from this ship and proceed to the surface of Janos. I'm afraid that does not help your case in defending the claim that you had nothing to do with the sabotage incident. You had better have a good explanation for this negligent oversight."

Most of the occupants of the bridge chuckled or smiled at Grannison's play acting but Keanyn was more sober. He commented about Dek's latest allegation. "That man is becoming more than a nuisance. Remember, folks, he has power behind his threats. He and his team were sent here by the Legion. That makes him more dangerous because he is an idiot with clout!" He turned to look at Mac and addressed her with, "Lieutenant Commander Stinson, what is the latest on Lindsey's dealings with Dek?"

"I just spoke with her last night right after Dek made that announcement and she said that he had been keeping her at arm's length for the last two days," responded Mac. "When I asked her why she thought that was, she gave me a forlorn smile and said that he told her that her attention toward him seemed disingenuous and that they should, perhaps, take a break from each other."

"That doesn't sound like the clueless Commander Dek we've come to know. He's not clever enough to spot insincere flattery from a politician let alone a beguilingly beautiful woman," stated Grannison.

Keanyn interjected, "I think it's safe to conclude that someone is feeding Dek information and, in this case, observations. Does anyone remember the name of that skulking sixth member of their team?"

Carl Burdgess excitedly spoke up, "I believe it's something like Ratchet, no, no." He became even more excited as he searched for the right name. Then, a light went on in his brain—figuratively anyway—and he assuredly proclaimed, "Raschkit, that's it, Raschkit!"

"You're exactly right!" stated JA exuberantly. He added,

"I don't mind telling you that I've caught him trying to connect to our communications system. He said he was only curious to see how some of the new and innovative technology worked, but you don't learn that by tapping into private 'in ship' communications. And that is what he was attempting to do."

Mac pulled her auburn locks back into a ponytail, then let it fall loosely around her face and shoulders. Something that had become a bit of a mannerism for her but one that always caught the attention of the captain. Whether she did this to playfully tease him or just as a habit, Keanyn couldn't figure out. But he enjoyed it nonetheless.

The science officer related her own run-in with Raschkit. "Not only has he been trying to decipher our communications, JA, but I've observed him at my station attempting to get into my storage locker where I keep readouts of some of my data from time to time."

"I think we can agree that he is a sneaky little snake we need to keep our eyes on," noted Keanyn while he gave a glance Mac's way.

"What little snake are we talking about now?" queried Robert as he entered the bridge.

"That weasel from the IA investigative team. You know, Robert, the one who's always on his vid comm," declared Grannison, who had returned to his pilot seat.

"Oh, you mean Raschkit?" proclaimed Robert. "He's certainly a piece of work. I did some background checking on him. Did you know he was picked up by IA and given a plea deal for a case the Legion's Anti Code Theft division had against him?"

"Can't say I did," said Keanyn giving Robert Porter a mischievous grin. "I'd say, that's more in your line of work."

Robert grinned back at the captain. He began to explain further about Raschkit. "It seems our little weasel had been hacking the ACT's records on a certain case dealing with the supplying of codes between the Legion and the head of state from Raushdon. The Raushdonians had agreed to supply the Legion with some of its—shall we say—less than upright business tactics."

"You mean their con artist negotiations?" interrupted Mac, whose time spent lately with Saffaw had demonstrated his species' particular abilities.

"Exactly!" said Robert. "They had only agreed to the arrangement if the transferring of the information was deeply coded and they were exempt from prosecution. The reason the Legion wanted the information was not to have a legal weapon to use against the Raushdonians, but to use their methods when negotiating with less-than-honest opponents. Raschkit's brazen attempt to steal codes from the very agency set up to prevent such action was extremely ironic. Therefore, the Legion thought they could put his talents to better use in working for them, resulting in the aforementioned plea deal."

Captain Mathews sat up straight in his command chair and declared, "That means our little weasel really is a little weasel and he's been feeding Dek's misinformation back to IA on Earth."

"Most likely," stated Robert. "But, I think he's been filtering it with bits of clarification so as not to put us in a bad light. That doesn't mean he is on our side. It just means he knows what a pompous airhead Dek is and he knows the Legion's aware of it also. If he fully supported Dek's accusations it might denote a desire on his part to undermine our mission which would, certainly, negate his plea deal."

"Well, that's a bit more encouraging," said Mac. "We might not need to pay so much attention to him now."

Keanyn shook his head in some doubt saying, "I wouldn't ignore him completely. He seems to be influencing Dek to back off from Lindsey's attention. Robert, do you think we might talk to Raschkit and persuade him to encourage Dek to give her another chance?"

The chief of security looked thoughtfully at the captain and offered this comment, "It is an idea to seriously consider, but it will have to be done very carefully and if anyone can do it, it's ND."

"With that, our shift is coming to a close," announced Keanyn. "If you three don't mind, I would like to see Lieutenant Commander Stinson, Commander Loche, and Lieutenant Commander Porter in my quarters in fifteen minutes."

A hardy, "Aye, aye," was returned by all three.

As the bridge emptied of its personnel, JA and Carl Burdgess approached the captain. JA was the first to address him, "Sir, since it will be some five minutes before the secondary bridge crew mans their posts, Lieutenant Burdgess and I would like to say something. Permission to speak freely, sir." He was obviously nervous but Lieutenant J. A. Philpot had come a long way from his cadet days before the "Swamp Maneuver." He may have been nervous, but his words showed confidence and determination.

"I'm all ears, JA," affirmed Keanyn, adding, "You can suspend the formalities. We're just friends here."

As always, JA was calmed and reassured by Keanyn's words and demeanor. He continued in a more relaxed manner, "Carl and I have been present on at least two occasions now when you have discussed what seems to be investigative activities on the part of you and several members of the command staff. You try to downplay it, but it seems clear that you have a team of officers looking intently into the sabotage plot."

Keanyn was a bit surprised that they had put two and two together. He thought that he and the rest of the team had only made it look like they were just curious and anxious—like everyone else—to have the issues resolved and the perpetrators brought to justice so that they could continue with the mission. He had forgotten how clever JA could be. Carl was no dummy either. He decided that coming clean was the best thing to do.

"You're right, JA, we have formed a team of officers, including all three of our crack security agents, to get to the bottom of this sabotage incident and try to prevent another one, which seems imminent. The IA team has no clue what's going on, both from the standpoint of our involvement or where the insidious plots actually originate. That's really a good thing. It keeps them out of our way so we can operate unimpeded."

Carl broke into the conversation, "I can only imagine the chaos Dek would create if he had an inkling of what was actually going on."

The three of them laughed as they pictured Dek charging headlong into the scene like a herd of wild horses. Keanyn spoke as their mirth died down, "You heard me ask Mac, Grannison, and Robert to my quarters. We are at a critical point in our investigations. I might even say we are ready to bring it to a conclusion and I want to work things out with those three and have a meeting with all of the team shortly afterword. I'm not bringing you in as part of the team. It's too late to bring you up to speed on everything. What I would like you to do is join me in these next two meetings and offer any suggestions you feel will help. I believe you both have the intelligence and the ability to observe that could greatly aid us."

Both JA and Carl were surprised and flattered by the captain's invitation and responded with, "Of course we will, sir!"

Keanyn added with a jaunty grin, "And, by the way, you can drop the sirs and misses. We're all part of a team during our meetings. First names only."

Carl and JA looked puzzled at first, but as their minds accepted the idea of being on level ground with the bulk of the command staff, their visages broke into huge smiles. Keanyn noticed and gave them a cautionary sign and said, "I'm sure you two will enjoy this new status, but don't get too comfortable, we will be covering a lot of information you won't fully grasp. Just concentrate on what you can comprehend and answer any questions even if you don't understand all the details."

JA responded with what was now a very sober demeanor. "I completely understand, sir—uh—Keanyn. We might be just a group of friends, not officers of varying rank, but we must still show respect."

"Exactly so!" confirmed Keanyn with a thumbs up. He added, "Now, let's get to my quarters because it's getting down to crunch time."

When Keanyn entered his quarters, the three who were already there looked up and immediately shot highly inquisitive glances his way. Robert Porter found his voice first, "Well, to what do we owe the pleasure of the company of these two fine officers?"

"You are always the consummate professional, Robert. Nothing ruffles your feathers," stated Keanyn. He then explained why JA and Carl were there and further offered his reason for making the decision to include them. "I told them we could not include them in the team as full members, but their intelligence at ciphering out our activity, yet keeping it secret, made me feel that we could use them as advisers."

Mac spoke up, "I have to admit that I've been keeping my eye on these two ever since we nearly revealed our activity on the bridge recently. I could tell they had suspicions so it doesn't really surprise me to see them here."

"I can't claim the same observational skills as our science officer," noted Grannison, "but I now wonder how many others might have picked up on our activities."

Robert observed, "Regardless, let's see how we can make use of our new additions. I just received a message from Salfrod and he was able to convince Ansmed to pay us a little visit."

"Have you got an ETA on that?" questioned Keanyn. "We're going to need time to set up our plan."

"Not to worry," stated Robert. "Salfrod assures me that it will take nearly one whole Saffo V day for Ansmed to get his crew up to speed on the situation and another three-quarters of a day to prepare a visit to our ship. This gives us a total of nearly eight days," he paused, calculated the timeline, then corrected his previous statement. "Well, actually, more like seven and a quarter to prepare for his visit."

Grannison questioned Robert, "I thought we had agreed on Salfrod telling Ansmed that it would take ten to twelve days before we could make an attack in order to push Ansmed to make a decision to come aboard the *Mall* ship to make a trade and avoid a fight?"

It was now Mac's turn to inject a comment, "We also agreed that Ansmed is not the type to be coerced. And he would certainly never back down from a fight. His motive for coming on board this ship will merely be curiosity."

"That's exactly right, Mac!" said Keanyn with assurance. "If Salfrod has done his job properly, he will have piqued Ansmed's curiosity to the point that he can't resist checking things out for himself. Remember, he has a significantly large ego."

Carl Burdgess and JA had been listening intently to this exchange and, while they didn't understand everything, they had formed some definite ideas. It was Carl who spoke up first.

"If I have put enough of your conversation together, I would most definitely count on this Ansmed character to have something more than curiosity as a motive."

JA concurred and added, "You've painted a picture of a crafty but violent person who won't stop at having his curiosity satisfied when he comes aboard. If I were you, I'd be prepared for anything from kidnapping to murder."

As he finished his statement, JA and Carl looked firmly at the four others in the captain's quarters. They, in turn, gave surprised but respectful glances at the two newcomers.

Robert spoke up, "Once again, Keanyn, you have proven to be an excellent judge of character. These two have cut to the chase of this situation and shown us that they can't be duped into believing that Ansmed's visit will have a simple solution. Well done, gentlemen."

Both JA and Carl humbly bowed at the commendation but maintained their confident demeanor.

"We have certainly not been kidding ourselves in the matter of Ansmed's determination to see our mission not only halted, but entirely wiped out!" declared Grannison emphatically. "We have no delusions that he will come to the ship with, merely, passive intentions." Keanyn further commented, "Be assured. We will be prepared for action when he arrives."

"Even so," remarked Mac. "We can't foresee every scenario. Ansmed is, indeed, crafty, as you said, and he may have something up his sleeve we don't yet see."

Robert brought up the reason for them being there in the first place. "Was there another reason for this meeting other than getting JA and Carl's input, Keanyn?"

Keanyn answered with an affirmative nod, then addressed everyone. "I want to make certain of our plan, but I wouldn't mind getting our new addition's viewpoints and suggestions. They've already shown keen astuteness and their observations could prove enlightening. Are you ready to hear the plan, gentlemen?"

This time it was Carl who spoke first. "JA and I are all ears, Keanyn. We can't wait to hear this plan, especially if it is going to bring an end to Ansmed's terrorism and sabotage."

"In a nutshell, gentlemen, our plan is to get him lulled into thinking that he has nothing to fear from us as far as repercussions are concerned. We just want him to think that we just want to get his uncle, the ambassador, back. We have not given him any reason to believe that we hold him responsible for the A deck sabotage. He may suspect that we feel he has something to do with it but don't have any proof. Also, if Salfrod has done a good job, Ansmed will give him back to us saying that he can't trust him because he suspects he is still regretful of the A deck incident and would end up siding with us."

"That sounds like Salfrod is a high-class con man," stated JA. He scratched his chin in contemplation and continued, "I assume you gave him some very good training?"

Robert informed JA and Carl of Salfrod's schooling in con artist education. "Would you consider Saffaw a prime instructor?"

Carl Burdgess was incredulous as he declared, "You have

entrusted a Raushdonian with the vital information you have and then put him in charge of mentoring Salfrod in duping our enemies? You have either lost your minds or are even better con artists than he is! And that's saying something."

"Now, that is exactly the reaction I had expected out of the rest of you when I suggested including Saffaw on our team," Keanyn proclaimed. "But Robert nipped that in the bud when he acknowledged the reasonableness of my suggestion and explained why."

Robert smugly replied, "And has my reasoning not proved true? Saffaw has demonstrated a previously unheard-of dedication to the success of the mission of the *Cosmic Mall* starship."

"Whatever the case," noted JA. "There is no doubt that Saffaw is the best teacher Salfrod could have had to learn how to bamboozle anyone."

They spent the next fifteen minutes giving JA and Carl more details on how they planned to detain Ansmed and stop any further sabotage.

"What do you think would happen if you fail to keep Ansmed on the ship?" JA inquired.

The others hesitated to answer, but Mac was not deterred. "I think it's pretty certain that if Ansmed succeeds in departing from this ship, it will, first, not be without violence and he will most certainly retaliate once he gets back to his ship, the *Hawk*!"

"Do you have a plan for that scenario?" asked Carl.

"Not exactly," said Keanyn. "We do have several ideas we've been working on, though."

Carl spoke hesitantly, looking at Mac as he did so, "I believe I can steer you to a possible scenario that I just formed this minute. It involves something I overheard Mac and Edward Butler discussing not long ago."

Mac interrupted with annoyance, "I suspected you and JA have been eavesdropping on me and others from bridge command. While it was just a feeling, I couldn't shake it. I guess you two know a lot more about our operations than you have let on. I can bet I know what 'discussion' between Edward and I you are referring to as well."

Keanyn held up his hands, palms out, to head off any confrontation and said, "All right, All right! I understand your anger and frustration, Mac, but JA and Carl are here to lend some help. However they obtained the information, they might have some very helpful ideas that could prove to be advantageous. Might I suggest that we proceed to Robert's quarters where, by means of communication with Cheng, I have summoned the rest of our team?"

They all agreed and filed out of the captain's quarters to discuss what they hoped would be a final resolution to the volatile situation facing them.

Commander Ansmed Kleek gazed at his two Legion-trained scientists with undisguised anger and shouted, "You assured me that our highly advanced transport masking system was exclusive and undetectable, and now you say that the command staff of the *Mall* ship may be on the brink of discovering how it works?" He was so infuriated that his face looked about to explode.

The older of the two scientists meekly replied, "I'm sorry, sir, but we felt confident that the use of a newly discovered and extremely rare substance as the catalyst for the new system would prevent anyone from uncovering it as our secret ingredient, so to speak. At least, not for a very long time."

"While you, Professor Winslow, and your partner, Dr.

Mmbunggoo, are highly intelligent, you are, by no means, the most intelligent creatures in the galaxy. Whatever ideas you have come up with are not exclusive to your super brains!"

As Ansmed said this, his voice continued to rise and his face turned blood red again. He finally stated, "Guards! See to it that these two idiot geniuses are put on house arrest. Keep a careful eye on them. I'm not putting them in the brig because I still need their brains, inferior though they've proven to be."

All of the Sabotage Investigative Team, plus two, were gathered at Robert Porter's meeting room in his quarters at the end of the corridor connecting the shaft leading to the bridge and the entrance to the mall, just opposite ND and Stenn's quarters. While larger than his living quarters, the meeting room was strained to capacity with eleven individuals and only ten chairs.

Keanyn chose to stand as he was chairing the meeting. He spoke to open the proceedings, "My friends, you all know JA and Carl, but their inclusion in this meeting does not mean that they are full members of our team. They have shown themselves to be keen observers of our activities and have contributed some excellent observations and ideas. Therefore, I have asked them to serve as advisers to us at this critical juncture in our investigations. They haven't been informed of all our activities, but they know enough to give us valuable insights."

When everyone agreed to the additions of JA and Carl, the meeting got underway with Keanyn asking Carl, "During our discussion, prior to coming here, you said you had a possible scenario based on a conversation between

Mac and Edward you had overheard." There were rumblings of anger from the five who had not been at that meeting. Keanyn quickly squelched it, saying, "I know that raises your ire, but the eavesdropping of these two has already proven to be beneficial so hear them out. Carl, what's your scenario?"

Carl was a bit hesitant as he began. "Well, Keanyn, for one thing, I said it is a *possible* scenario. It's dependent on what conclusions, if any, they have drawn from pursuing Edward's thought."

Cheng interrupted, "It seems that it is imperative to know just what Edward and Mac discussed before we hear any more from our two advisers."

Everyone agreed to this suggestion so Keanyn gave the floor to Edward. He began with, "I was merely curious about an idea I had developed that I felt could only be confirmed by our brilliant science officer."

"You already buttered me up sufficiently enough to convince me to consider your idea, Edward," stated Mac with a grin.

Edward acknowledged her comment with a nod in her direction. He continued, "I have been very interested in the transporting process and the extent to which its technology might be taken. As a navigator, I am involved in the transporting of individuals as well as inanimate objects, since I have to provide coordinates to which the one transported is sent. The recent advancement to hyper-speed transports from Ansmed's ship, and Mac's ability to improve on it, have really piqued my curiosity. So I approached her with the thought of examining the transporting capabilities to include an entire starship."

To say that the reaction to this statement was vocal disbelief was an understatement. Even the normally stoic ND was flabbergasted. She declared, "My goodness, Edward! What kind of drug did you take to come up with that idea? It took us decades for the Legion's physicists and engineers to successfully develop the basic transporting of the first inanimate object, a pen. Now you want to jump to an entire starship?"

"My initial reaction was very similar," said Mac. "But then I thought. Once they accomplished that first transport, they had the basic formula and all it took were a few adjustments to be able to transport the first living, breathing entities. The time that took was mere weeks. Now, our transport technology has come considerably forward. Maybe we need to start thinking bigger."

Grannison had been trying to recall something this discussion had triggered in his mind. He suddenly remembered and said, "What about that attempt they made about twenty-five years ago to transport a shuttle-craft from a starship orbiting fifty-four Piscium B? It was a disaster and they never tried again."

"That was just it!" exclaimed Mac. "They quit on it. I thought of that failed test too and I dismissed Edward's idea instantly. But he was persuasive and insisted that if they hadn't given up so quickly, they may have found a solution. I agreed to take a look at it, just to get him off my back," she finished with the surprising declaration. "Well, 'lo and behold!' as my father would say. If there ain't something to it anyhow!"

Cheng voiced her thoughts, "You mean to say that the transporting of an entire starship is possible? I am familiar with the botched attempt with the shuttle. That's one of the lessons I received in my training as shuttle deck commander and it was a shame what they did to that poor ship. I'd certainly hate to see that happen to a vessel as big as this one."

"I can't, categorically, say it's probable, but it is definitely possible," said Mac. She looked resolutely at the others and added, "I was just about to take my findings and ideas to Chief Engineer Davis at the end of our shift on the bridge when Keanyn asked Grannison, Robert, and myself to meet him in his quarters."

Keanyn, whose reaction to the idea Edward had posed to Mac had been much less incredulous than the others, looked very thoughtful as he spoke. "I don't pretend to know just where you and Edward are going with this idea, but I think I know what Carl might have in mind."

He looked at Carl and asked, "If I guess this right, Carl, your idea involves not just any starship, but the *Mall* ship in particular. Right?"

Carl answered, "I had heard about the high-speed transporting that brought the stowaway on the ship. That was not a result of eavesdropping, but a well-substantiated rumor that had spread throughout the ship. That's actually when I started trying to catch any snippets of conversation between the command staff, especially those from the bridge.

"Then when you, Keanyn, and the others were discussing your concerns after Commander Dek and the rest of the Legion investigators came on board, JA came to me and asked if I had noticed how you had tried to make the discussion sound like general curiosity and concern. He said it seemed more than that to him.

"I agreed and told him how I had suspected some kind of effort on the part of a number of the bridge command to look into the sabotage in an organized manner and how I had been listening for clues. We decided to combine our efforts and bounce ideas off each other.

"I know I've made this answer a little long, but I thought it was necessary to explain how I got to the point of thinking that there might be an advantage, in this particular situation, to being able to transport this vessel instantly at some critical juncture. I also think that is what Edward has in mind as well."

Edward shot a look of total surprise at Carl. *Had he really been that transparent, that easy to read?*

He addressed Carl with newfound respect saying, "I'm either that careless or you are very observant and intuitive. I suspect the latter."

"Yes," he continued. "I felt that the ability of a starship to 'pop' in or out of place could be extremely advantageous in certain circumstances and I anticipated the *Mall* ship would find itself in such circumstances. I also knew that Mac had solved a number of difficult problems already and if anyone could figure this one out, it would be her. So I brought the idea to her."

"He was placing a lot of confidence in you, Mac," stated Grannison while glancing at his younger half-brother. "My little brother has a knack for challenging people to extend their abilities beyond their previous boundaries. It appears you accepted his challenge."

"What convinced you otherwise?" inquired Robert.

Instead of answering Robert directly, Mac addressed Grannison again, "Your brother is not only persistent but very persuasive. He countered my argument with the fact that I had solved, a previously, unsolvable dilemma with the development of Trilliatide propulsion. Then he asked if the basis for transporting had been established with the transporting of the pen all those years ago, weren't those fundamentals used to speed up the process to the point of animate transport? He concluded by noting that I had used the same principle in developing the new propulsion from already established science as my basis." She paused and sighed. She concluded with the outcome of Edward's persuasion. "I had to admit, he had some good arguments, though I was still doubtful of success. If nothing else, it was worth the effort to prove him wrong." She gave Edward a broad grin and a playful punch on his arm. He responded with a look of mock hurtfulness and rubbed his arm as if it really hurt. Mac gave a chuckle and continued, "To my surprise, I found that he was right. The ability to transport an entire starship is possible, at least, theoretically."

As most in the room stared open-mouthed at her statement, Keanyn took the opportunity to move the meeting forward to other matters, saying, "As astounding as all this is, we have no application of it to the problem we are currently dealing with. May I suggest we keep it on the back burner while Mac and 'Stokes' work out the kinks? We need to establish a more firm plan B in case Ansmed slips through our net."

Just then, a call came in for Keanyn. A coded message from Salfrod. "Ansmed is coming aboard!"

CHAPTER TEN

NEGOTIATIONS

"I'm not an idiot, Salfrod," declared Ansmed after he had been convinced to go to the *Mall* ship to negotiate a trade. "If you think I am so naive as to believe that Mathews and his cronies don't have an ulterior motive for wanting me on that starship, you are sadly mistaken."

Salfrod was ready for Ansmed's suspicion. He grinned and said, "Of course not, commander. I'm well aware that they would prefer you to be under lock and key in their brig than make any kind of hostage exchange. That is just a ruse as I'm certain is the case with you as well."

Ansmed had a thoughtful look on his face as he said, "No doubt, Salfrod, no doubt. But I've just had an idea that will require the minds of my two scientists to tackle. And, if they are on the top of their game, will guarantee that there will be no lock and key for Commander Ansmed Kleek!" He said this as if he was the epitome of cleverness.

Keanyn quickly informed the rest of those in the room about Ansmed's imminent arrival and the room erupted in confusion. Many expressed their fears. Cheng was the first to be heard, "I thought it would take him at least another day before he arrived!"

Stenn voiced his concern, "We haven't got a solid back up plan. If we can stall Ansmed for a couple of hours, Robert, Mom, and I might be able to come up with something."

"Keanyn, do you think I should still consult with Stokes about the transporting?" wondered Mac.

There were several other comments made rather loudly so that Keanyn needed to shout and wave his arms to get their attention and quiet them down. When he accomplished that he spoke. "First, we do have a plan for Ansmed. We just don't have a secondary one that's complete. So it would be good for the security team to try to complete the backup as quickly as they can." The security trio nodded their agreement and informed Keanyn that they would keep him updated on their progress.

Keanyn moved to point two. "Mac, go ahead and enlist Stokes's aid on the transport issue. Once you convince him that you and Edward aren't crazy, get him started on figuring out the engineering aspects of it, then take your leave. We're going to need you while we are dealing with Ansmed."

He now made an assignment that utilized the two newcomers, showing the confidence he had gained in them. "Carl, you and JA have demonstrated a tremendous ability to observe behavior, collect information, and decipher what that information means. I think we can use you in this endeavor." They were all smiles as Keanyn outlined his plan. He started by addressing JA. "Your language and communication skills can be used to set up a ruse to distract Commander Dek and his team from butting their noses into our operation. I'm pretty certain I can have General Beckton send a bogus message from Janos about some new delicate information he has and that he would feel better if Dek and his team came down to Janos to handle it as they are more adept at diplomacy than he is. That should be more than enough flattery to get Dek there. To delay them further, JA, I'll have one of the general's contacts on the planet act as the informant. He will need to speak in a language only you can translate. Don't worry about being accurate, just makeup anything that will keep our good Legion investigators occupied chasing their tails."

Keanyn then turned his attention to Carl, "I do believe that Robert wishes you had been in security, Carl. You would flourish there. That being said, I'd like to ask Robert, ND, and Stenn if they wouldn't mind taking you with them to help figure out the backup plan. I think you could come up with some excellent suggestions."

He looked at Robert who responded with, "If you hadn't brought it up, I would have insisted on it." ND and Stenn both agreed and Keanyn sent them off to get started.

"Time is of the essence!" he said as they departed. Then he added, "That goes for you as well, Mac. I'll contact Stokes and tell him to expect you and Edward in engineering."

Cheng chimed in saying, "What have you got for the rest of us, Keanyn?" She, Grannison, and Saffaw—who had been strangely quiet—had been patiently waiting their turn.

Keanyn looked quizzically at the Raushdonian mall manager but addressed all three with the words, "The rest of you can come with me. If you remember each of your parts in the plan, you'll still need to carry them out with just a slight adjustment to make up for the absence of Mac and the security trio. I'll discuss that with you on the way to the shuttle bay."

When they arrived, they discovered that Salfrod had been able to delay Ansmed for about an hour. Keanyn took the time to find out what was making Saffaw so silent.

He and Saffaw went into Cheng's office for privacy. Keanyn asked Saffaw to sit down in one of Cheng's specially ordered chairs she had imported from China.

Saffaw was still untypically quiet as Keanyn began to address him.

"I'm sure you know why I want to talk to you. I don't think I've ever seen you silent for more than two seconds. Now I haven't heard so much as a peep from you for the last hour and a half! What's bothering you, Saffaw? Is there something playing on your mind? If we can't have you at your normal level of activity, your effectiveness in helping us reach a successful conclusion is greatly in doubt."

Saffaw nervously ran his fingers through his copious locks of reddish-brown hair and looked over at Keanyn who was leaning against Cheng's desk. His facial expression was one of deep concern as he replied, "We Raushdonians have always been known as a fun-loving but hard-working species. We also have a knack for pulling off clever business deals, though not with any malice. It's simply the joy of the process that we love.

"That reputation is reasonably accurate and we aren't interested in trying to deny or defend it. But I have recently come into possession of some information that has shaken my confidence in that assessment of my character. In fact, in the essence of who a Raushdonian is!" He was becoming more agitated as he spoke and his expression became more worried.

He continued, "When I heard this information, I knew I would have to report it to you because it is vital to our investigation. It involves a rumor I had heard about six or seven days ago. When Robert asked me to consider joining the team, he asked if I had heard anything that seemed unusual. I told him something I'd been told about the Sharlee, kwark. It seems she had been acting down and depressed. Quite uncharacteristic for a Sharlee.

"Later, I received a request from kwark to hire a number of Sharlees to help in certain areas of the mall. Then I learned that some of those very Sharlees had bribed or used intimidation to force employees to leave the mall and, thus, open up positions for the Sharlees. This information really concerned me because their strange behavior was so baffling. I decided to hire them because we actually needed them now but, more importantly, to keep an eye on them and try to figure out what was behind their odd behavior."

"What did you find out?" Keanyn eagerly asked.

Saffaw replied with even more concern than before. "That's just it! I just found out as I was leaving for this last meeting something that shook me to my core and brought on the silence you witnessed." He paused and took a long shaky breath. Keanyn remained quiet, not wanting to upset Saffaw further.

After several seconds Saffaw continued, "I know for certain who Ansmed's undercover agent is on the ship. It is kwark!"

While the investigative team had suspected it might be

a Sharlee, they thought that kwark may have been coerced or threatened to hide or aid another Sharlee who had transported onto the ship as Salfrod had but, unlike Salfrod, had gone undetected. This news about kwark herself was extremely unsettling.

Keanyn recovered from the shock and asked Saffaw, "What makes you so certain it is kwark?"

"Because my operative heard her discussing the blow she had given Salfrod when he came on board." He paused giving Keanyn a look of frightful certainty. "She was talking to one of her fellow Sharlees named Waulooq who seems to be the chief one among the eleven that I hired. After she had told of silencing Salfrod, my operative, who had planted a bugging device in kwark's room, quoted her as saying, 'I couldn't let that stowaway identify me as his contact. Ansmed would have my head if that happened.'"

It was Keanyn's turn to take a deep breath, after which he said, "I hadn't counted on this, but it does give us an ace in the hole when we confront Ansmed. But why does this make you so melancholy?"

Saffaw replied, "If Sharlees can act so completely out of character, what about Raushdonians?"

Keanyn was puzzled at Saffaw's answer. He couldn't understand why the unpredictable behavior of one particular race would affect the exuberant mall manager so profoundly. He asked, "Why would their behavior have such a detrimental effect on you?"

"That's just it!" said Saffaw. "It's not just one Sharlee but it's the entire group of twelve. Look, Keanyn, Sharlees are like Raushdonians in that they are known to have a very well-defined character. They are, as a species, known for their fun-loving nature. That's not simply a generalization, but it is a dominating trait of each and every one of them.

It's not that they're incapable of serious behavior or unable to make mature decisions. It's that, when not having to act seriously, they prefer to be rather silly. And they especially like to have fun when they are in groups. So when twelve Sharlees are together and behave in a sinister and even violent way, something is seriously out of whack!"

Keanyn was beginning to see where Saffaw was going with this and questioned him. "Are you saying that this has caused you to fear that your species, who also possess a well-defined behavioral pattern, might somehow experience a total flip in personality?"

"That is correct, Keanyn," Saffaw replied sadly. He added, "To think that one's very identity could change overnight is extremely disheartening. You might actually cease being who you are!"

"I understand your concern but I think you are overreacting a bit," said Keanyn. "Let's reason on this for a minute. For species who have such a solid identity of character as the Sharlees and Raushdonians, would some mysterious force be the reason that would cause them to change their deeply entrenched personalities all of a sudden?" He stared intently at Saffaw as he awaited his answer.

After several seconds of thought Saffaw noted, "That doesn't seem to be a very reasonable explanation. But there are a lot of strange things in the universe." He sounded a bit more hopeful but not convinced.

Keanyn tried to wedge the gap wider between Saffaw's hope and fear. "Remember, we have another very plausible explanation for the change in the Sharlees' behavior."

"What's that?" asked Saffaw.

Keanyn spread his arms out and gave a look of obvious realization, declaring, "Why, the same one that has been the guiding force behind the whole mess we've been dealing with, of course!"

"You mean Ansmed?" asked Saffaw.

"Naturally," Keanyn said. He then explained the logic of his conclusion.

"We already know that Ansmed has been able to convince a number of individuals to not only accept, but also adopt his view of Earth and the *Mall* contribution. He has also indoctrinated them in the violent conduct needed to destroy this ship and, thus, Earth's reputation. He even maneuvered Salfrod, whose opposition to our cause was much more passive than his, to attempt an act of sabotage. It goes without saying that he convinced his own influential uncle to believe he was a changed person and cause him to, unknowingly, perform certain actions he used in framing the ambassador. I am certain he could brainwash a few Sharlees into attitudes and actions contrary to their nature."

Saffaw visibly relaxed, sighed, and stated, "That does make sense. He seems driven to destroy our mission and has proven to be ruthless in his efforts to succeed." He paused in thought as he ran this conclusion through his mind. After a minute he looked up at Keanyn and said, "I'm glad we had this talk, Keanyn, I believe I am now ready to proceed with my part in the plan regarding Ansmed."

"Good," said Keanyn. "We need you and everyone else to be ready if we are going to succeed. And there's still no guarantee!"

As they returned to the others gathered around Cheng at the shuttle control center, Keanyn received another coded message from Salfrod. He looked grim but determined as he conveyed the message to the others.

"Salfrod informs me that Ansmed, Ambassador Calluran, Chief Secretary Omnivie, and Salfrod himself are boarding a Janovian shuttle on its way here. He couldn't stall him any longer and since he had to convince

Ansmed to come aboard in the first place, he doesn't want to risk having him back out now."

Cheng reported that the Janovian shuttle had just lifted off and would be landing on the deck in twenty-two minutes and seventeen seconds. She looked up from the controls and said, "If there are any changes in our plan we need to implement, now would be the time to let us know, Keanyn."

He had a look of concentration and his hands were on his hips with his eyes gleaming as he spoke, "Lady and gentlemen! We could very well be about to bring our efforts to a conclusion in the next hour or so. Keep to your original assignments. I'll call Mac to see how soon she can be here to make her announcement that we have figured out how Ansmed has been able to transport without detection. We will confront him about it and, per his reaction, move forward from there."

At that, the party of four lined up to greet the shuttle as a welcoming committee.

When the shuttle landed and opened its port side doors, the three officers and the mall manager stood in a straight line prepared to greet the exiting occupants. As the first figure appeared in the open portal, Captain Keanyn Mathews stepped forward to address the individual who proved to be Chief Secretary Radule Omnivie.

Keanyn saluted the secretary as a gesture of respect and said, "It is an honor and a pleasure to welcome a dignitary as important as you, chief secretary." While this visit could end up being controversial, it didn't hurt to butter up the opposition with flattery. It wouldn't work on Ansmed but it probably would with Omnivie.

"It's good to finally have the opportunity to see your most unusual starship, Captain Mathews. And I appreciate your kind greeting," stated Omnivie. "May I present my three fellow passengers?"

As he said this, Ansmed appeared at the top of the ramp leading down from the shuttle's open portal. He was wearing an official-looking silver-plated breast piece with a six-sided shield-like insignia emblazoned with a red and brown hawk in flight. Its wings were fully spread. Just above it was the word HAWK boldly embossed in gold, which brightly reflected the lights from the shuttle deck. If Ansmed had been looking to make an entrance with a strong statement, he had accomplished it.

Secretary Omnivie nervously wiped imaginary dust from the arm of his jacket as he turned to announce Ansmed's arrival. Gesturing with his right arm-like appendage toward the open portal he declared, "May I present, Commander Ansmed Kleek. The captain of one of Saffo V's most advanced star fight—ah, I mean, star cruisers, the *Hawk*! Commander Kleek leads a crack team of dedicated crewmen. His interest in our meeting comes from the fact that he is Ambassador Calluran's nephew."

The long-winded and horn-blowing introduction was not lost on the four individuals who made up the welcoming committee. It was also impossible to miss the slip-up that nearly referred to the *Hawk* as a starfighter instead of a cruiser.

Keanyn replied to the declaration of Ansmed's credentials with a slight smirk and a direct stare into Kleek's eyes. "We are quite aware of Commander Kleek's position in our upcoming discussions and are looking forward to his insights and opinions. He is most welcome on board this vessel."

"I am flattered by your acknowledgment and welcoming words, captain, and I look forward to our discussions," stated Ansmed with a similar smirk.

Saffaw leaned into Cheng and whispered in her ear, "You might want to get a shovel. This stuff is getting deep."

She gently poked Saffaw in the ribs saying, in an undertone, "We may need a bull dozier before it's over."

Secretary Omnivie now came to the last two occupants of the shuttle and announced their arrival together.

"Now, to the reason for our meeting. The one you formerly knew as a stowaway who has abandoned our cause and has become sympathetic with yours. Former *Hawk* crewman, Salfrod."

There was an obvious note of disgust in the secretary's voice accompanied by a derisive glare from Ansmed, but they kept it civil and, apparently, ruffled no feathers.

Secretary Omnivie continued, "Finally, here is one you have been missing for quite some time. Your previously beloved head liaison officer, Ambassador Yahnsoof Calluran!"

Keanyn silently took note of the expression "previously beloved," but made no outward acknowledgment of it. What he did was smile broadly, walk up to the ambassador and warmly shake his hand while saying, "It is a great relief and joy to finally see you again, Mr. Ambassador. I hope you are well and have been treated fairly."

"I am no worse for wear, captain. I greatly appreciate your concern and can assure you of my good health."

Keanyn turned to Salfrod and addressed him with the words, "It's good to see you, Salfrod, though the manner of your exit from this ship three days ago makes me doubtful if you truly are in support of our mission."

Salfrod gave Keanyn and the other *Mall* ship personnel a sheepish look and said, "I deeply apologize for that, Captain Mathews, but if I would have tried to explain why I wanted to take a shuttle down to the planet, you would have denied me."

Grannison broke into the discussion with, "Don't explain now, Salfrod. Explanations are to be left for the negotiations which I have been selected to chair. I suggest we retire to the meeting room of our head of security, Lieutenant Commander Robert Porter. Our shuttle bay director, Lieutenant Cheng Wong has made sure that we will be comfortable and supplied with snacks and beverages."

It had been decided when making their plans for Ansmed's visit, that they would meet in a smaller room than the more spacious shuttle deck conference room. It could seat up to thirty individuals at dining tables and had extra room for serving tables, a speaker's dais, and milling about. This gave Ansmed and his allies too much room to cause trouble. Robert Porter's chambers would keep everyone cozy and easy to keep an eye on.

As Salfrod greeted the *Mall* contingent, he whispered to Keanyn, "I have some very important information to give you as soon as we are alone." He said this with a smile on his face and with his head nodding so as not to give the nature of his comment away.

In just a matter of minutes, they arrived at the security chief's quarters. As they entered, Grannison directed each one to their seats. He began with the following statement, "Ms. Cheng and gentlemen. You will notice a tablet of paper and a writing implement at each of your seats. You are also supplied with small vid screen devices on which you may take five minutes to enter points you desire to discuss or resolve during these negotiations. Refreshments are on the table at the end of the room opposite me. Comfort facilities can be found through the door to my left. Now, if there are no objections, I declare these negotiations officially opened!" At that, Grannison took a gavel and pounded it firmly on the gleaming block of oak in front of him.

"Hang on to your hats!" exclaimed the irrepressible Saffaw to the smiles and frowns on the faces of each side of the table.

JA and his two guards had landed on Janos just minutes before Ansmed and his party took off. JA had made his way to General Beckton who was staying at Earth's embassy on Janos. As soon as he was welcomed by the general, he got down to business.

"General, we have little time to spare. Have you requested that Dek and his team come to Janos to help you solve a problem?"

The general was amused at JA's abrupt manner, realizing that he was nervous because of the heavy responsibility he had been charged with. Keeping this in mind, he responded to JA in a quiet, inoffensive tone.

"Yes, Lieutenant Philpot. I told Dek that we had encountered a Bregman from Mallussa who was an undercover agent in the Janovian SDG, or secret deployment group. He had been working in the Saffo V embassy as a janitor while keeping tabs on the diplomatic staff. When Ansmed and his crew showed up, their suspicions were heightened."

"Thank you, sir," said JA as he softened his tone, realizing how directly he had addressed the general. "I hope I'm not out of line?"

"That's perfectly all right, lieutenant," stated Beckton.

"I appreciate that, general," said JA gaining confidence from Beckton's words. He continued, "I'd like to ask you how much of what you told Dek was true, and what is a Bregman from Mallussa?"

The general laughed as he recalled how he had

fabricated a story made up of both truth and deception. He was still smiling as he explained. "First of all, a Bregman is a member of a small tribe of humanoids with reddish-brown skin and seven fingers and toes per hand and foot. Their digits possess tremendous flexibility and strength, giving them the ability to climb and hold onto just about anything.

"Mallussa is the remote area they inhabit. It is made up of dense forests and a vast open plain known as the Cuawnin, in their tongue. In the center of the Cuawnin is a large lake, fifty-seven miles wide and 118 miles long. It is inhabited by 247 different kinds of fish and mammals. The Bregmen catch several species of them using their powerful digits.

"As for the story of our particular Bregman, it is mostly false." There was a mischievous grin on Beckton's face as he continued, "He was, indeed, employed as a janitor in the Saffo V embassy, but as far as being an undercover agent, Bregmen do not possess either the ability or inclination to pull that off. What they do possess is a talent for acting and, therefore, are prime candidates for our purpose. His name is Soolehmein"

JA inquired, "How did you pick, uh, Soolehmein? I thought you were going to pick one of your team to impersonate someone who had important information for us."

"I had seen him act in a play at a theater near the Saffo V embassy and he was amazing. When I found out that he worked at the embassy, I figured we might be able to use him in some way. Then when I heard what Keanyn wanted me to come up with, I immediately thought of Soolehmein," explained the general.

JA was still concerned about the language aspect of their plan and stated, "General, sir, I don't know anything about the language of the Bregmen. Do they have a tongue of their own or do they speak the common language of Janos? If so, that poses a problem. That language is fairly well known and someone from Dek's team will probably know that what I interpret will be bogus."

The general calmly replied, "The Bregmen speak a dialect of Teemun, a little-known tongue spoken only by about thirty thousand of Janos's 6.2 billion inhabitants. Very few people outside of those who speak it are familiar with it. Soolehmein says he can teach you the basics so that when you interview him, you will appear to understand it. How much time do you think you'll need?"

JA was surprised by this difficult assignment but gathered himself and replied with mock confidence. "As long as the words and sentence structure are *very* basic, an hour or two should do."

"Let's make it an hour to an hour and a half," declared Beckton. "As you said yourself, we have very little time!"

If JA was nervous when he first landed, he was nearly a wreck now. Not only was he going to have to fabricate a story to tell Dek, he'd have to do so with a language he didn't know.

Robert, ND, and Stenn, with the addition of Carl Burdgess, were feverishly trying to come up with a backup plan in case their initial one failed. They had no time for research or the consideration of various ideas. With Ansmed and his group already in discussions with Keanyn's team, they needed a plan NOW!

"We need something that will cover either a peaceful departure by Ansmed or a violent one," stated Robert with more than a little anxiety.

Stenn noted, "The end result to either of those cases must be the detention of Ansmed on this ship! We can't have him running loose to bring destruction on our ship and who knows what else."

"I think we would agree that a peaceful attempt to depart is practically out of the question when it comes to Ansmed," stated ND.

Carl decided to add his two cents. "How are you planning to detain him in the first place? If he is so prone to violence, wouldn't you need a number of armed crewmen to do so?"

"That is exactly what we have planned," stated Robert. "They are being kept in two of the adjoining quarters to my own where the negotiations are taking place."

"How many exactly?" queried Carl.

"Twelve," noted Robert. "They will come to my quarters as soon as they receive a signal from Keanyn from his comm unit. Six of them will enter the room and six will be posted just outside the door."

Carl was looking thoughtful as he said, "That will work as long as Ansmed stays in your quarters. But what if he doesn't wait to make his move until after they leave your quarters to have a meal or retire to sleep if the negotiations are prolonged?"

Robert looked at Carl and said, "We are pretty certain that Ansmed will show his hand fairly early in the negotiations."

"I'm of the mind to arm the four of us and go to the discussions as members of the negotiating team," offered Stenn. He concluded with, "That way we can stay with Ansmed if or when he leaves Robert's quarters without arousing suspicion."

ND supported Stenn, saying, "I agree. That is a very

plausible solution. Even if Ansmed was able to smuggle a weapon on board, it would be a four-to-one advantage for us."

Carl noted, "That is a reasonably good plan. It seems, though, from what I have heard about Ansmed so far, there is always an unknown factor involved. I still don't trust his willingness to so easily be persuaded to negotiate. After all, this is the one behind the disastrous A deck sabotage."

"I believe," said ND, "that Carl is even more suspicious than our good chief of security. And that is saying something!"

Robert brought their meeting to a conclusion. "With so little time to waste, I say we implement Stenn's plan with the addition that we talk to the twelve crewmen just before we enter my quarters and have them discreetly follow if the negotiators adjourn the discussions for later."

"When you first came in here and told me what you wanted to do, I was ready to call Doc Karushkin and tell him to come and get you because you were talking out of your head," said Chief Engineer Stokes Davis to Mac. "Now, after you've made a completely insane idea sound possible, I'm wondering if I don't need Doc's help too!"

Mac laughed softly before speaking, "Don't worry, chief. I had the same reaction when Edward here first proposed the idea. But isn't that the way new and innovative ideas are treated? A lot of those ideas eventually become reality. What did we on Earth think of traveling beyond the speed of light, let alone transporting, before the Legion came to Earth?"

Stokes pondered as he answered, "I guess that makes sense. After all, some of the things I've discovered just by tweaking a few things in engineering were kind of unbelievable. Then there's something I said to Robert before we even launched that reminds me not to dismiss any idea out of hand."

"Does that mean you will give it a try and see if our idea has an engineering solution?" asked Edward anxiously.

Chief Davis stated, "Nothing ventured, nothing gained!"

Mac and Edward both smiled as they shook Stokes's hand and took their leave.

After they exited the engineering deck Mac turned to Edward and said, "I've got to get to Robert's quarters as fast as I can. I've got an important statement to make."

The negotiations had been tense but only mildly confrontational. Salfrod and Ambassador Calluran had been placed in separate quarters. The very ones that currently contained the twelve crewmen awaiting Keanyn's sign. Salfrod already knew about them but the ambassador had to be informed of their purpose. Ambassador Calluran thought it was a good idea since he was well aware of his nephew's volatile behavior.

At the negotiations in Robert's quarters, though, Keanyn was more concerned about Ansmed's lack of action. He would have suspected Commander Kleek to have already reacted to some of their accusations. Especially when Grannison brought up the fact that Salfrod had been transported to the *Mall* ship from the *Hawk* for the purpose of meeting with an undercover agent to carry out a sabotage plan.

The only reaction they got from Ansmed was for him to say, "How do you know for certain that he came from my ship? You said the blow he received from the 'mole' on your ship gave him amnesia. Therefore, how reliable could any information from him be?"

Grannison countered with, "It has been thoroughly substantiated that Salfrod was a member of the crew of your ship, not to mention that your own chief secretary has admitted that Salfrod was a former member of your crew. Our suspicions concerning you and your ship are perfectly reasonable."

"Not necessarily," countered Ansmed. "His actions could have been completely independent. I don't recall giving any order for him to be transported to this ship, let alone including him in any sabotage plan."

Cheng Wong spoke for the first time. "By your own words, then, you admit to having a plan to sabotage this starship."

"My views about the Earth's contribution to the Legion are well known by now and I continue to be opposed to this ridiculous venture," stated Ansmed with some heat. He calmed himself down and commented further. "There are many within the influential circles of the Galactic Legion who share these opinions and some have even resorted to aggressive actions. That does not mean that I nor any one of them have carried out any sabotage toward this starship.

"With that being said, I must conclude that any action taken by Salfrod must have been initiated on his own. As a member of my crew, he would have naturally shared my sentiments toward this *Mall* project. He, undoubtedly took his feelings to a more active level, independent of any orders I gave.

"Then, when he was injured upon arrival on your ship and experienced amnesia, he was more malleable to having his opinions concerning your ship altered to acceptance of your mission."

"The only flaw in that argument," noted Keanyn, "is the fact that, in order to carry out this 'independent' plan, Salfrod would have had to partner with the undercover agent on board this ship. Partners in a venture such as the complex sabotage scheme carried out on our A deck would need to work closely together, requiring them to know each other to some degree. How do you correlate that to the fact that the planted agent on this ship went to such violent means to prevent Salfrod from seeing them in order to know who they were?

"In addition," continued Keanyn. "If this was all an independent act by these two individuals, how do you explain that in a few months, another individual from the *Hawk* transported to this ship and, with the aid of the undercover agent on this ship, did indeed successfully carry out the heinous act of murderous sabotage we experienced?"

It was evident that Keanyn had hit a nerve with these logical questions. But, with a monumental effort, Ansmed brought himself under control and answered, "As I had nothing to do with these plots, I can only conjecture the answers to your questions, captain. One explanation might be that there was at least one more who shared Salfrod's zeal but was more thorough in planning. They could have learned the identity of the agent on your ship, contacted that person, and worked out a new plan. That would have taken some time and so it was some time later before they were ready to carry it out."

Ansmed sat back in a nearly reclining posture with a smug and satisfied smile.

It was Secretary Omnivie who now broke into the discussion with some irritation, saying, "Gentlemen, gentlemen! Excuse me, Lieutenant Wong. We did not come here to have Commander Kleek put on trial. Yet you have persisted in grilling him about his involvement in something you have no solid proof for. We were led to believe that the purpose for these negotiations would be to make an exchange of Ambassador Calluran for this so-called undercover agent. Having agreed to that, it is no admission on our part that said agent was planted on this ship by anyone representing Saffo V. Our interest in this exchange is to question this 'agent' in order to administer punishment for their actions which besmirched the reputation of the good people of Saffo V!"

It was at this moment that Mac and the four from the security team gained access to the room.

Mac immediately spoke. "Excuse the interruption, but I have just come from engineering to report that Chief Engineer Stokely Davis and I, Lieutenant Commander and Science Officer McCardle Stinson, have just deciphered the high-speed transporting method being used by Ansmed from his ship, the *Hawk*. Thus, explaining how Salfrod was transported to this ship undetected and how they were able to transport Ambassador Calluran from here to the *Hawk*."

The room erupted in denials from the Saffo V duo and accusations from the *Mall* ship's negotiators.

Grannison was finally able to settle everyone down with the frantic pounding of his gavel and his commanding, deep-voiced shouts. When calm returned, he addressed the other newcomers. "Do the rest of you who have just entered have any statements? If not, then identify yourselves for our two visitors."

Robert, who had been chosen to be their spokesperson, spoke up. "I am Commander Robert Porter, head of security for this starship and, along with me are my civilian colleagues, Stenn and his mother, ND. I have been handling a security issue that delayed us from arriving on time."

Both Ansmed and Omnivie look puzzled and some-what bothered by the addition of so many and the chief secretary voiced their concern.

"Mr. Chairman, my colleague and I feel uncomfortable with so many representatives of your cause greatly out-numbering just the two of us representing Saffo V. Is there some compromise we can come to?"

Grannison smiled apologetically as he replied, "Mr. Secretary. I do apologize for this sudden addition of so many. May I suggest that we take a break for a meal at one of the fine restaurants in the mall? This will allow us to relax and give the Earth negotiators an opportunity to make this situation less intimidating for you. It can also give you an opportunity to see why the *Cosmic Mall* is a positive addition to the entertainment and recreation possibilities so needed within the Legion."

Ansmed made a very surprising reply to Grannison's invitation, "I can't deny being curious as to why this 'mall' has the appeal that many have expressed. I suppose that seeing it for ourselves might answer that . . . or not."

"Then I declare a recess of two hours. We will reconvene at six p.m. Earth time for three more hours of negotiations if needed," announced Grannison with a firm bang of his gavel.

As they left the room, Salfrod tugged on Keanyn's sleeve and motioned with his head that they should move to the back of the line. He was nervous and anxious as he addressed the captain in a low voice. "I wish we could have had a more private opportunity for this but I don't think I can wait for that now."

"My goodness, Salfrod!" exclaimed Keanyn as quietly as he could. "You're scaring me a bit. Not to mention that

Ansmed's behavior is totally baffling me. What do you have to tell me?"

"Something that might explain Ansmed's behavior," claims Salfrod. "I didn't actually cause the delay in our departure from Janos. I didn't know how to explain it to you quickly in our coded communication so I will now.

"Just as we were about to board the shuttle, the two Janovian physicists Ansmed had managed to recruit to his cause ran up to him saying they had made another breakthrough. Ansmed quickly quieted them and the three of them went into the shuttle hangar. They came out about an hour later and, as he approached the shuttle, I saw him look at something in his hand, smile, and put it in his jacket pocket. Also, when he did so, I think I caught sight of a holstered weapon. He's got something sinister up his sleeve, Keanyn."

Keanyn replied as if his fears had come true. "I knew he had trouble on mind for his visit here. I just thought he would reveal it while we were in negotiations. That makes me think of something. Can you find out the whereabouts of Larindo kwark? I feel she's going to be involved in this somehow."

"Right away!" said Salfrod. "I'll ask Saffaw where I might find her."

"Better, yet," remarked Keanyn, "take him with you. I'll think up some excuse for the absence of you two."

The meal the negotiators were treated to consisted of the juiciest filet mignon any of them had ever had. It goes without saying that this was the only filet the duo from Saffo V had ever had.

To the surprise of all in the Earth party, Ansmed genuinely praised the flavor and texture of his steak. Secretary Omnivie was, virtually, speechless as he took each bite and looked up to the ceiling with a face of pure joy. One thing they couldn't criticize about Earth was its food.

No one questioned why Salfrod and Saffaw weren't around. Perhaps it was because the colorful owner of the *Cosmic Mall* had graced them with her presence. Clarice Pickle had been contacted by Saffaw, when he had learned of their dinner destination, and she was waiting to greet them in the restaurant's lobby.

"You couldn't have made a better choice for steak in the entire galaxy, ladies and gentlemen," she greeted. Then she added, "Due to the important stature of our guests and the vital nature of their discussions, no expense will be spared on the forthcoming meal. All the courtesy of the owner of this fantastic shopping and entertainment edifice—who, by the way, is me—will be extended to your all-important entourage."

Clarice was always 'on' and ready to promote anything that could advance her reputation as a first-class entrepreneur. Besides the succulent steak, Clarice proved to be enough of a distraction to keep Ansmed from noticing anything out of order.

When they had all finished eating and engaging in small talk, Clarice invited them all on a tour of the mall, even though all but two of them were quite familiar with it. When Keanyn was able to get to her side, he discreetly whispered in her ear, asking, "What are you doing? We only have a two-hour recess and we are already an hour and forty minutes into it. Your tour will take the rest of the day."

Clarice addressed the rest of the group, "My friends, the captain has just told me of your time constraint, but I believe that your discussions—if I understand them correctly—will be enhanced by our two guests from Saffo V getting a first-hand experience of the incredible showcase all around them. I promise to shorten my normal VIP tour by two-thirds. You can then all get a good night's sleep and resume your negotiations with a fresh perspective in the morning."

Everyone turned to look at Grannison Loche who, as chairman, was responsible for presenting any changes of procedure before them for consideration. Although taken by surprise, he confidently raised his head and voice to address them. "Ladies and gentlemen," he began.

As he did so, Keanyn grabbed Clarice and gently guided her into a secluded seating area of the restaurant. He looked her straight in the eye and with thinly veiled wrath said, "Are you nuts! Keeping those two overnight was the last thing I wanted to do! That opens up all kinds of possibilities for them to cause chaos!"

"Believe me, Keanyn. This was not my idea." He looked totally confused as she began to explain, "Do you remember when I took that short break during dinner to 'refresh myself'?"

He nodded dumbfounded and she continued, "My bracelet had just vibrated. It is not just a piece of jewelry — it doubles as a warning device by vibrating when Saffaw sends me a signal that he needs to talk with me. He never uses it unless it's an emergency or he has an extremely important message. Since he had already told me how vital it was for me to meet your group at the restaurant, I knew he had something equally as vital to tell me."

"And he told you to make sure that you took us on a tour in order to keep Ansmed and Omnivie overnight?" asked Keanyn incredulously.

Clarice answered with confidence. "Yes, but not quite that simple. He said he had located the one you were looking for and that if I invited you all on a tour, that would go directly to the center court on the first level, you would find them and he could take it from there."

"Oh boy!" Keanyn said. "Now I'm trusting Saffaw to bring this delicate situation to a head!"

CHAPTER ELEVEN

ANSMED'S AGENT UNMASKED

When they returned to the group, Grannison had managed to bring the rest to agree on an abbreviated tour of the mall that would extend their recess by one and a half hours. This would leave them one and a half hours to resume their negotiations. They had also agreed to a two-hour extension if the talks appeared to be moving toward a resolution.

They had also reached a compromise on any added participants. Only Mac could remain and the four in Robert's group would have to wait in an adjoining room until called, one at a time, to participate.

Keanyn excused the absence of him and Clarice by saying that they had also discussed keeping her tour short and only hitting the high points. Clarice had added the use of the pre-programmed transit pods to speed things up even further. Instead of Clarice narrating the tour, she would have her mall manager, Saffaw, do the honors, with her giving brief supportive comments.

The tour began by meeting Saffaw at the Whale fountain in front of the mid-mall anchor store, Creshkas, a men and women's clothing and accessory store from Tadmore in the Gamma Cephei system. They proceeded from there directly to the third level center court to give everyone a panoramic view and to marvel at the cascading waterfall.

It's to be noted that the visitors from Saffo V were impressed by the fact that the mall could house such natural wonders as the waterfall and the botanical gardens together.

"Of course, they have to be meticulously maintained," noted Saffaw. "We have a crew of knowledgeable and experienced employees headed by our two honor graduates from the Legion's advanced schools. Doctor Stella Steel with her degree in plant science and her assistant the, Sharlee Larindo kwark, who possesses a master's degree in botany."

Saffaw and Keanyn noted Ansmed's reaction to the mention of kwark and saw a slight stiffening of his posture and a nervous tick on the left side of his face. It would not have been noticed by anyone who wasn't looking for something. But they were.

Saffaw continued his narration, "We will now proceed to the second level center court and then onto the first."

When they reached the first level, the Jal bead pool was on its dazzling display of multicolored iridescence as the water from the cascade thundered into it. Clarice was effusive in her comments with such expressions as, "I can't begin to tell you how deeply I was affected by my first view of this dancing wonder of light and color. I was overcome by a wave of joy and peace to the point of fainting away!"

"I'm sure we are all profoundly affected by its shimmering beauty, Mrs. Pickle," affirmed Saffaw. He gestured to the hedges surrounding the pool and then to the plants and shrubs spreading out on a lawn that made up a carpet-like expanse on each side of the waterfall. Trimming those shrubs were Stella Steel on one side and Larindo kwark on the other. They had arrived some ten minutes earlier from the third level.

They hadn't noticed the presence of the tour due to the loud roar of the water and the deep concentration of their labor. Ansmed immediately noticed kwark and, this time, his reaction was obvious. He quickly straightened his stance and began to turn away as if to leave, saying, "I'm sorry, but the sound and continuous flow of the water has caused a reaction that necessitates my being excused."

Most everyone hid their smiles except Keanyn, Saffaw, and, surprisingly, Clarice. Saffaw took the bull by the horns and dropped the bombshell, "Ansmed, I think you know one of our hard workers over there."

Ansmed stopped in his attempt to get away and turned to look directly at Saffaw with unveiled malice, saying, "Why, whatever do you mean, Wheerie?" His addressing Saffaw by his species rather than his name showed his contempt at being maneuvered into this position.

Saffaw was not deterred. He turned to Larindo kwark and shouted, "Excuse me, you two who are working so hard over there, I would like you to meet our distinguished guests from Saffo V."

The pair of workers stood up smiling, but when kwark caught sight of Ansmed she froze in fear.

All but four of those gathered there were clueless as to what was happening. To them, this was just going to be an opportunity for an interview with the ones in charge of the beautiful plants and flowers of the mall's landscape. That view was shattered with the next statement by Saffaw.

Looking from kwark to Ansmed, Saffaw pointed toward kwark and stated loudly, "I think we've found your undercover agent on our ship, Ansmed."

Before anyone else could speak, Stella Steel shouted, "What's going on, Lari? What does he mean by calling you an undercover agent? Is this another one of your little games, Saffaw? If it is, I think it's in poor taste."

"No game, I'm afraid, Stella," stated Saffaw with a sad expression. He turned back to Ansmed and asked, "Do you have an answer for my accusation?"

"Wait a minute!" declared Grannison. "Are you saying that you know the identity of Ansmed's mole on this ship? The one who knocked Salfrod over the head and nearly killed him? Our very own kwark?" As he said this, he was shaking his head in disbelief along with several of the others.

"Yes, he is, Grann," said Keanyn. "He told me he had found out she was the mole just before we greeted our two visitors earlier today. His evidence was undeniable, but I had no time to brief anyone else. From what I observe, though, it seems that Stenn and Mrs. Pickle already knew this or had a pretty good idea."

Stenn, who had been standing at the back of the group to keep an eye on Ansmed, stepped forward and spoke, "While I was on Janos scoping out the embassy, I saw a reference on one or two occasions to Ms. kwark as having supplied Secretary Omnivie with information concerning the Trilliatide engines."

"How could you have done that? I always kept those

communique in my personal valise!" blurted out the chief secretary. He added pointing at Stenn, "I know who you are. You're that janitor at the embassy who said he was studying diplomacy. You went with—" he stopped, looked at the rest of the group, and pointed at ND saying, "with her! Madam Dunford from the Agricultural Alliance. Or so she said."

"I thought there was something familiar about those two, but they kept standing in the back of the group with their faces turned away," stated Ansmed. "Who are you?"

"She's my mother," said Stenn, casually. "She and Robert here"—he noted pointing at the security chief— "we all work in security on this ship. In fact, we do a lot of undercover jobs. . . . And, yes, you did have those communique in your 'unlocked' valise."

Finally, Ansmed threw off all pretense and shouted at Omnivie, "You complete fool! How many times did I tell you those papers must be kept absolutely secure? You weren't even allowed to look at them. I had them sent to you instead of me so as not to arouse suspicion."

Ansmed made a sudden move, putting his hand behind the *Hawk* shield on his chest, and pulled out a laze gun. That was met by Robert and the other three with him pulling their weapons and aiming them at Ansmed.

The twelve crewmen who had been casually following the negotiators fanned out in a semicircle behind everyone and brought their weapons to bear.

Undaunted by this display of weaponry aimed in his direction, Ansmed slowly turned his aim toward Larindo kwark and accusingly said, "If you had not revealed the full purpose of Salfrod's visit on the *Mall* starship to him and bash him over the head when he tried to see you, you could have calmed him down and taken him to your quarters until enough time had passed so that we could have transported him back to the *Hawk*."

Mac remarked on Ansmed's last statement, "We wondered why you didn't transport Salfrod back to the *Hawk* immediately. Later, while we were trying to figure out your high-speed transporting system, we discovered that the super speed at which one is transported causes a spike in body temperature so that one couldn't be transported again immediately without the danger of getting a life-threatening fever. You would need to wait at least one hour."

Ansmed looked derisively at Mac and replied, "I don't know how you figured our transport system out so quickly, but if kwark had not reacted so impulsively, we could have gotten Salfrod back on our ship. Once you discovered him, we couldn't take the chance to get him back. We needed to take time to train another agent to do the job Salfrod was supposed to do. But your thoughtless reaction, kwark, put us in a precarious position. I should have known better than to recruit a Sharlee."

Cheng Wong broke in. "If you don't mind. I would like to know why, of all the races, you chose a Sharlee?"

Ansmed admitted, "You said it yourself. 'Of all the races.' Who would ever suspect a Sharlee? The hard part was convincing them to act in a manner totally foreign to their nature.

"I did that by telling kwark here that, while she and her friends thought everyone else enjoyed their good-natured antics and frivolity, they were actually laughing behind their backs at them. They never took them seriously. Couldn't credit them with a single serious or mature thought. I had to spin this line of thought to her at least a hundred times before she began to give credence to it. But, boy, when she did, she took it all the way."

Larindo kwark spoke as Ansmed's duplicity began to dawn on her. "Are you saying that all the information and examples you used to convince me were lies? When you first started to change my way of thinking I felt sorry for you. You seemed very unhappy and I couldn't understand that. I thought I could help you, but your relentless insistence on the fact that Sharlees were maligned and disrespected eventually made an impression on me.

"That was not enough, though. You manipulated me to recruit eleven other Sharlees to the cause. We were even willing to use violence because you said people weren't laughing with us, but at us. You said, to them, we didn't matter!" As she finished, she hung her head in shame.

Stella Steel had been listening to this long enough. She stepped next to kwark and pleaded, Lari, please tell me this isn't true. You are not only my assistant, whose work I take very seriously, but my best friend. We were in school together in the same dorm! We've worked side by side ever since graduation! You let me give you the nickname, Lari. It would break my heart if all this were true." She started sobbing but spoke through her tears. "You know I and everyone on this ship not only enjoy your playful antics but admire the beautiful work you've done with all of these flowers and plants. Why, you've even heard them praising you as a true artist. I couldn't do my job without you! YOU ARE IMPORTANT! YOU MATTER!"

With one exception, everyone was profoundly moved by Stella's sincerely emotional plea.

However, Ansmed was aggravated at the waste of time and showed it with his words. "Yes, yes, how touching, but irrelevant. I assume you want to apprehend me and either hold me for a tribunal or execute me. Personally, if I were you, I'd go with the second option. It's quicker and saves a lot of money."

"You're not just a murderer, but a psychopath as well!" stated Mac heatedly.

"It's easy for you to despise me and think of me as some kind of degenerate!" returned Ansmed equally angered. His face contorted into a mask of hate as he further ranted. "But, before your pathetic planet was somehow invited by the Legion to make a contribution to become a member, I could sense that you didn't belong with us. I don't know what got into the Supreme Command Council and the Selection Committee to invite you. Then, even more absurdly, they accepted this gaudy display of rank hedonism you call the starship *Cosmic Mall*! The only thing it can contribute to the Legion is greed.

"As far as you're concerned, kwark, I probably made a mistake in recruiting you. Your failures have cost me dearly. It appears that I will be incarcerated until they probably decide to execute me." He shrugged as if accepting the inevitable and trained his weapon more squarely on kwark and said, "But, before that happens, I think I will eliminate you as a problem."

He didn't fire immediately, but, inexplicably and calmly, put his left hand in his pants' pocket while continuing to keep the laze gun on kwark. Everyone else kept their weapons aimed at Ansmed.

Stella once again spoke and said, "This is insane! Won't someone stop him? That madman is going to kill Lari and blame her for his problems. What a coward!"

Larindo kwark looked fondly at Stella and said, "You've always been there to defend me, Stella. You are a true friend. But I am partly responsible for the deaths of all those from the A deck disaster, though I didn't know the full intent of Ansmed's plan. I deserve to die!"

"I didn't know someone actually cared for you,

kwark," said Ansmed with a condescending grin. I'm sure you would hate to see anything happen to her."

With that, he shifted his aim to Stella and began to fire, but kwark was quick and leaped in front of Stella as the laze beam hit her square in the chest.

The action froze the ones ready to return fire, but as they did, they found themselves firing into thin air. Ansmed was nowhere to be seen. Bewilderment and confusion reigned as everyone tried to figure out just what had happened.

"What was that?" shouted Robert frantically. "One minute I had him in my sights and when I pulled the trigger, he was gone!"

A few others wondered if, since so many had fired their high-powered laze beams at Ansmed all at once, they vaporized him.

Mac gave her thoughts on that idea.

"The laze guns are fairly potent, but you would need a lot more than a dozen or so to generate the power to completely vaporize someone. In fact," she stated, "it would take the power of at least fifty weapons in one concentrated beam to accomplish—" She had missed the final result of Ansmed's laze gunshot and as she looked in the direction of kwark and Stella, she gave a sharp cry of fear and anguish. She saw their crumpled forms lying on the grass verge of the shrubs they had been trimming.

"Oh no!" Mac screamed as she feared the demise of her friends. She barely kept herself from collapsing before gathering herself and rushing to them.

Just then, Salfrod ran up to Keanyn and with consternation in his voice, said, "That's what I was worried about! I remember who those I told you about seeing with Ansmed were."

"Who?" asked Keanyn, as he was still recovering from the events that had just occurred.

"I had seen them a few days before I was transported here as a stowaway," explained Salfrod. "Someone told me that they were Janovian scientists recruited as mercenaries to develop some new breakthrough they had come up with as a theory. They didn't know what that theory was, but I can make an educated guess that it had something to do with the new transporting system." Salfrod arrived at his conclusion. He spoke as if this revelatory thought had just dawned on him. "When I was transported to this ship, I was told that I would be the first to experience an awesome new discovery in the field of physics. I was going to become a pioneer in the field!"

Stenn, who had been standing nearby and overheard the comments of Salfrod, said, "So you think those two Janovian scientists were the ones who developed the new high-speed transporting system as well as whatever new gadget Ansmed just used to make his getaway." He said this as a statement and not as a question.

"But how could that be done without taking the time to enter coordinates?" asked Keanyn. "If you just pushed a button without coordinates you would end up in oblivion."

Salfrod had sussed that out and said with a wry smile, "I believe that the device Ansmed had slipped into his pocket was preprogrammed with the coordinates to which he intended to transport."

"He may be a psychopathic criminal, but he's also a clever and dangerous character," observed Stenn with a look as if he had a nasty taste in his mouth.

Keanyn was wringing his hands in frustration as he spoke with growing fear, "Now we have the situation we were desperately trying to avoid! Ansmed has slipped through our net and, be assured, he will not merely be satisfied with getting away. You heard his contempt for our mission. A person who has committed mass murder won't balk at destroying this ship! We have to be ready for some sort of retaliation. We have to round up the team ASAP!"

Meanwhile, Mac had reached the two fallen botanists and immediately checked Stella, who was lying halfway under the Sharlee. She found that she had just been stunned by having kwark's massive weight crash into her when she was felled by Ansmed's laze ray. She was just beginning to stir as Mac cradled her head in her lap. She fluttered her eyes open and groggily spoke, "What . . . Uh, what happened?"

"You were knocked unconscious for a few minutes, that's all," Mac assured her smiling.

Stella Steel looked doubtful as she responded, "I seem to recall that there was more to it than that. In fact, what am I lying under?"

She managed to sit up and look toward her feet. When she caught sight of Larindo kwark lying across her lower body with a laze hole through her chest, she gasped and began to sob, saying, "I remember now. She jumped in front of me and took the shot meant for me!" She began wailing. "You loving, loyal, fool of a friend! You thought we saw you as too frivolous and unimportant. The laughing stock of the entire ship!" She paused as her sorrow got the better of her, but, after about thirty seconds, she was able to continue. "You were anything but unimportant or a laughing stock. You just sacrificed yourself for me. What bravery and selflessness! Two qualities that only the best people—and Sharlees—display! I love you, my dearest friend."

Mac released her tender hold on her as Stella leaned

down as far as she could and engulfed Lari's oversized head in her arms and rocked back and forth with uncontrollable sobbing.

After about a minute, she felt a stirring in Larindo's body. She stoped and looked directly into kwark's half-closed eyes as they slowly opened and gazed into Stella's with a clear smile. She began to speak with a quiet but strong voice. "He had me believing that I had no true friends in the whole galaxy. He said your friendship was merely a veneer for pity. I just wanted to prove that Sharlees could be serious when it mattered." There were tears running down her face as she finished.

"I never imagined it would result in the death of hundreds. He lied to me all along but, after the deaths, I felt trapped and kept quiet. That was my worst crime."

She began crying quietly, then, suddenly gasped as a surge of pain wracked her body. When it subsided, she gathered all her remaining strength and put her left hand on the side of Stella's face, softly caressing it, and whispered, "You are the truest and best friend I could ever have. . . . Ah!" She grimaced with another shot of pain but rallied herself for a final time. Her voice was so weak that Stella had to lean down as close to her mouth as she could get as Lari haltingly said, "Whenever you plant a flower . . . think of me and I will be right there . . . to help you pack the soil around it." She smiled broadly, as only a Sharlee could, and slowly dropped her hand to one side, as a last long breath left her lips.

Her body relaxed into death as Stella Steel and all of the others who had gathered around were not ashamed to shed tears for their fallen comrade.

After a few minutes, Keanyn brought the group back to the present.

"I'm sorry to have to say this, but we need to get to Robert's quarters and plan what we are going to do to combat Ansmed's next move. And we need to do it quickly. It appears that our adversary had his departure planned and whatever his intentions are from that point, he won't waste any time about putting them into action."

"One thing we can count on, Keanyn," said ND, "it will include violence! Violence that will most certainly be focused on us!"

CHAPTER TWELVE

SURPRISE! SURPRISE!

When they reached Robert's meeting room inside his quarters, their group included newcomers Carl Burdgess and Stella Steel. JA was still down on Janos but Keanyn used his private comm channel to tell JA to get back to the ship, STAT!

Another addition to their group was Clarice Pickle. Keanyn had suspected she knew far more than she let on and as they all crowded into the room and sat down or, once the seats were all taken, stood.

Keanyn addressed Robert. "I strongly suspect that in the case of Mrs. Pickle here, you have been keeping an extremely tight lid on her involvement in our little investigations."

It was ND who replied instead of the head of security, saying, "That was my doing, Keanyn. You see, Clarice is my aunt and, after the death of my father, Ronald Downing, his sister Clarice took me under her wing. When I took a shining to investigative and undercover espionage, she spared no expense to see that I received the finest training. Then, with the birth of Stenn and the untimely death of his father in a covert operation, Clarice saw to his training as well."

She appeared, somewhat, uncomfortable as she finished her reveal by saying. "My full name is Natalia Downing Rotterdam. Downing is, of course, my maiden name, and Rotterdam the name of my late husband, Sir Henry Clive Rotterdam, ACBI, Assistant Chief of British Intelligence under the European Alliance's Espionage Bureau. My aunt has always had her hand in our operations to one degree or another. She is an extremely intelligent woman and uses her lack of interest in anything outside of her financial empire as a cover."

Saffaw was wide-eyed as he declared, "You mean, all this time I've been working for a super spy!?"

Clarice answered, "I'm surprised I was able to keep that from your prying eyes. Maybe I should have taken on a career in acting. To have pulled the wool over someone as good at conning people as you are, Saffaw, is quite a feat. If I do say so myself."

Stella Steel was the next to speak up. "So you all are some kind of investigative team? What am I doing here?"

Keanyn had a sad smile as he looked sympathetically at Stella and said, "First of all, let me say, Ms. Steel, how sorry I am at the loss of your good friend, Larindo kwark. Her final heroic gesture and words of repentance have gained her an honorable legacy."

"I'm pleased to hear that you feel that way, captain. I'm still in shock at learning of her duplicity. You're right. She was my best friend and her sacrifice on my behalf proved her true loving nature. I hope the rest of the Sharlees involved with her will be as equally remorseful."

"I immediately had my assistant, Ross Carter, get several of his men to round up the Sharlees," stated Robert. "I injected a copy of the vid from the scene at the mall to Ross's vid comm and he just reported to me that the Sharlees have seen it and have promised to do 'service time' to make up for their behavior. None of them were involved in the sabotage plot."

"Service Time" was the name for punishment chores. Keanyn grinned mischievously and addressed Robert, saying, "I think a nice round of cleaning the Frothy Mugs latrine vents as well as those on all levels of the central court's comfort stations would be in order. Don't you agree, Lieutenant Commander Porter?"

Robert nodded his head in agreement with the same mischievous grin on his face and said, "That might be too good for them but I can't think of anything more appropriate."

Keanyn turned his attention back to Stella and apologetically stated, "I am sorry for the digression, Ms. Steel. You were asking why you have been included in our meeting. For beginners, there was no opportunity to drop you off somewhere else in our haste to get here. But I have been thinking that you could serve a vital purpose at just the right time but I'm not sure just what that is yet. In the meantime, you have earned a place in our discussions so feel free to comment whenever you feel inclined."

Stella Steel blushed slightly at Keanyn's acknowledgment of her, but spoke up despite that. "I thank you greatly, captain. I'm not sure what I can contribute since my expertise is in plants and flowers, but I will try to follow your discussions and something may come to me."

"We've already had excellent input from Carl and JA, whom you will meet as soon as he arrives from Janos," stated Stenn, who had been quiet till now. His comment was accompanied by a very friendly smile and an unusual look on his face as he gazed at Stella.

Stenn's odd behavior did not escape the notice of Saffaw or ND however. Both of their minds were racing to analyze what it could mean. Each of them had different lines of thought.

At that moment, JA burst into the room and announced, "Someone's got to meet Dek's shuttle when it arrives in the next fifteen minutes! He's on a warpath. I was able to deceive him for a good while, but he got suspicious when Rashkit kept agreeing with me about looking into the market stalls in Grelnad, the market town just outside the capital city, Wradovia. We were trying to convince him through my bogus contact that there was an undercover agent working for Saffo V and posing as a vendor in one of the market stalls. Since there are over 450 stalls in the market, it would take Dek an infinite amount of time to find the nonexistent agent and keep him out of our hair. When Rashkit, who didn't like Dek much anyway, had agreed to help us instead of Dek we figured we could keep Dek occupied for a good long time.

"But Rashkit agreed with my suggestions once too often and Dek started to think he was being maneuvered. That's when he said he was coming back to the ship to confront you, Keanyn. I left immediately and asked Rashkit to stall Dek as long as he could so I could get back to warn you. Rashkit just called to tell me they were on their way."

"That's all we need! Another complication," declared Keanyn. "We've got to take care of this quickly and before Dek has a chance to get to this room!" He pointed to Cheng and stated, "Take Grannison and Stenn with you and catch Dek and his cohorts as soon as they disembark from the shuttle. Grab Rashkit, who seems to be cooperating with us, and have him help. It's time to stop playing with Dek and put the proof of Ansmed's treachery right in front of him. Robert, give Grann your copy of the vid from the mall and, you Grann, make sure Dek and his men are convinced of who was and is behind all of the death and violence. Then tell him that, if he does not cooperate with our efforts to bring Ansmed to justice, we will offer him and his crew a lovely stay in our brig until this is all over!"

"Aye, Aye, captain!" was Grannison's enthusiastic reply.

Keanyn finished by saying, "We will be done here shortly and will proceed to the bridge where you can join us. NOW GO!"

When they departed, Keanyn quickly got everyone organized with a plan. He said, "We have no weapons on this ship, but we do have the strongest shielding system in the galaxy. That will buy us some time because, as sure as Saffaw could con the hair off a Larm, Ansmed will bring all his weaponry to bear on us."

"That won't last long unless we have help," noted Mac with a worried look.

Keanyn's response was to say to JA, "Get Captain Paxton on your mobile comm and have him call a red alert and bring his entire weapons system online. Also, have him position the Gator behind us by fifty clicks. That will make him appear less threatening to the *Hawk*."

ND broke in with the chilling observation. "You are setting us up as bait, Keanyn. Do you think Ansmed will fall for that and just come charging in?"

Keanyn answered, "You saw his behavior in the mall. He wants to destroy Earth's contribution so much that it's driven him to the edge of sanity and that makes him extremely dangerous."

"What about help from the forces on Janos?" inquired Carl.

"I was about to get to that," noted Keanyn. "Now that we have Ambassador Calluran back, I think we should use him to help us with the Janovians. After all, that's his job, and I have a feeling he'll jump at the chance to get back in the saddle."

"How do you plan to use him, Keanyn?" asked Robert.

The captain hesitated before answering, "He had established an excellent rapport with the government officials as well as the military command before he was escorted off this ship by Ansmed's men. I think that when he tells them who was responsible for his kidnapping, the Janovian military will be more than happy to help us defend ourselves."

Keanyn looked around at everyone and gave the order to dismiss to the bridge.

Once there, he received word from Dooley Paxton that he was taking the *Gator* to a position fifty clicks aft of the *Mall* ship and would await orders with his finger on the firing button. Just like Dooley to be ready for action.

While everyone was checking their readings to make sure everything was ready, Robert came up to Keanyn and addressed him in military terms now that they were on the bridge.

"Captain, I've just received word that the second agent Ansmed had placed on the ship has surfaced. It seems he hasn't heard from Commander Kleek in several days and, when he got wind of the events in the mall, he figured he'd been cut loose by Ansmed and turned himself in."

"What was his purpose here, commander? Did he say?" wondered Keanyn.

"He said he was in contact with kwark about sabotaging the climate control systems in the mall. He said that Ansmed wanted those visiting the mall to be made to feel highly uncomfortable," Robert returned.

"That seems rather tame compared to the kind of sabotage he had already perpetrated on us," remarked Keanyn with perplexity.

Robert explained, "My feelings as well when Lieutenant Carter told me. But he explained that with the violence of the A deck, coupled with the failure of something as simple as the climate control units, something that the visitors could complain about back at their home planets as eyewitnesses, the credibility of our mission would be destroyed."

"Not only can we not keep people safe, we can't even keep them comfortable," realized Keanyn with a forlorn shake of his head. He continued, "I've got to admit, that Ansmed is clever. Diabolically clever. What do you suggest we do with this second agent?"

Robert pondered the question for a few seconds before answering. "Well, Naryelga—that's his name—never began the actual sabotage. He had only gotten kwark to get him schematics of the system. He was not involved in the A deck catastrophe and he voluntarily turned himself in. The most we could charge him with is illegally gaining access to this ship for clandestine activity, i.e. a spy." He shrugged his shoulders and concluded, "Maybe place a guard or two with him and assign him some 'service time.'"

Keanyn smiled saying, "I trust your judgment, commander. But I will add that you don't make that decision until you speak to Naryelga first."

"Perfectly reasonable, sir," said Robert. "I will inform Lieutenant Carter to confine Naryelga to an available private quarters with a two-hour period each day for guarded exercise until we are finished with our current situation."

"Very good, Lieutenant Commander Porter," declared Captain Mathews returning the salute Robert had given him.

JA suddenly spoke, "Communication for Lieutenant Commander Stinson from engineering."

Mac punched the button that connected her with Lieutenant Commander Davis in engineering and said, "What have you got for me, Stokes?"

His excited reply was clear and direct. "We did it! We did it! You told me to enlist Patsy's help to figure out how to program the formula into the ship's mainframe and we've come up with something I really think will work!"

"You didn't put it into the computer yet, did you?" asked Mac anxiously.

Stokes replied, "No, of course not. We know we need your input to make sure it is sound from a physics perspective. It also needs to be run through simulations testing to be certain of its effectiveness. But it is essentially a solved formula that has a high probability of success. When are you free to add your insights and begin simulations?"

Mac replied with a nervous explanation, "We've got a potentially volatile situation on the bridge right now. But, if I had the time, I would get this thing working as soon as possible!"

Keanyn turned from the captain's seat and looked at Mac in the science station saying, "What's going on over there, lieutenant? We need your focus on the matter at hand."

Mac pressed a button on the arm of her chair that activated a small yellow light on the captain's wrist comm. This served as a secret summons to meet privately.

As Keanyn noticed the flashing amber signal he turned back, looked at Mac, and gave acknowledgment with a slight nod of his head. He addressed the bridge, "Science Officer Stinson and I have a most urgent matter to discuss that could greatly impact our current situation. Therefore, we need to meet privately for the briefest of moments."

They went into the power lift and locked it down.

"Was that Stokes on your comm unit?" began Keanyn.

"Affirmative!" returned Mac and added, "He said he has come up with a formula for the instant transporting of this ship and just needs my input and simulation testing to make it a go."

"How long will that take?" inquired Keanyn.

"Normally, the process would need several weeks of testing. My input as a physicist could take anything from a day or two to ten days, depending on the complexity of the formula."

"As you know, we don't have the luxury of time right now," said Keanyn. "I'm not sure how I could use it if it were up and running. I have an idea or two but nothing concrete. If I sent you down to engineering right now, how quickly do you think you could come up with something?"

Mac had been hoping he would ask her something like that. She smiled as she answered him. "Maybe an hour to check the formula and tweak some things. Then another hour for a quick simulation. If their discovery is as certain as Stokes made it sound, that should be enough time."

Keanyn looked thoughtful, took Mac by the shoulders, and looked resolutely into her eyes as he said, "You certainly are beautiful when you're using that brilliant brain of yours. Go to engineering and take your two hours. If you have a working solution by then, I promise to have a way to implement it against Ansmed." Then he leaned down and tenderly kissed her, stroking her hair as he did so.

She didn't resist and as they pulled away, Keanyn said, "You'd better get going, we can talk later."

He opened the door to the lift and stepped back out on the bridge as Mac pressed the down button. and the lift door closed as it descended to the bottom of the power shaft on her way to engineering.

All eyes were on Keanyn with some—like ND, Clarice, and Stella Steel—casting him knowing looks.

He cleared his throat as he said, "What are you looking at? We've got work to do."

Ansmed had no sooner set down on the landing pad at the Saffo V embassy when he was met by Ambassador Musslavo who was beside himself with fury. He approached Ansmed and angrily shouted, "Are you out of your mind, Kleek! Do you realize that you have put the entire embassy at risk? My position will be seriously in jeopardy and the representation of Saffo V on this planet could very well be terminated! What do you have to say for yourself?"

Commander Ansmed Kleek peered directly into the ambassador's eyes with a steely stare as he replied, "Maybe I am out of my mind, but if you want the Earth's disgusting contribution to come to an end, you're going to have to risk losing your precious position. I would have thought you realized that when you agreed to assist me in this operation. Besides, I don't care one bit about Saffo V's credibility anymore. Since the heads of state were cowered into accepting the Earth as a member of a Legion that has abandoned the high scientific standards it was built on, it is no longer the Legion I belong to!"

The ambassador turned his attention to Secretary Omnivie who had just disembarked from the shuttle. He was clearly not happy with his chief secretary and it was apparent by his comment. "I can't believe you allowed that murderous activity to take place on that ship, Omnivie! Can't I trust you to keep the interests of Saffo V in order? Which is your job to begin with!"

"Everything happened so fast, Mr. Ambassador," the secretary whined. "Those officers on the *Mall* ship had a trap in place to get Commander Kleek to acknowledge his undercover agent and implicate himself, and us as well, in the sabotage plot."

"How did you get away?" asked the ambassador.

Ansmed spoke before the secretary had a chance, saying, "I had a little surprise of my own ready for them. I got away before they could even react. I believe I'll keep the secret of my surprise unrevealed for now though."

Ansmed's pride couldn't prevent him from boasting. He was as he always had been. Self-centered and overconfident.

The ambassador turned back to Omnivie. "Is that how you got away too?"

"No, sir," replied the secretary. "I was actually taken into custody but not detained. Their security chief, Robert Porter, told me that they would allow me to return to the embassy but with the message that action would be taken to bring sanctions on Saffo V by the Legion and that they, the officers of the *Mall* ship, would put a bounty on Commander Kleek for his capture . . . or death!"

"They're just blowing smoke," stated Kleek confidently. "They need to go through the proper diplomatic channels in order to bring sanctions and as to the price on my head, that's something else they can't decide arbitrarily."

"Maybe they can't officially put a bounty on you. But, I don't think that will stop them from trying to liquidate you in any case," noted Ambassador Musslavo with a subtle grin. He addressed them both and said, "Now, just what are we going to do? Sit tight and wait for whatever develops? Which, I am certain, would not sit well with you, commander. Or we could contact our judicial officials on Saffo V and spin some plausible scenario to have them back us up against any action, legal or diplomatic, that is taken. Then there is a third option that I would be extremely reluctant in taking, but, as I suspect you, Commander Kleek, would not hesitate to implement."

Ansmed was hesitant but thoughtful, "If you are referring to a swift and determined show of force, that might have been my first inclination. But, I have learned patience. I've also seen the advantage of biding my time and striking when one has let his guard down. Besides, they will be expecting instant retribution and will be better prepared. If I wait, just a little, I will be the one prepared and I will blow their stupid ship into oblivion!"

What's taking Ansmed so long? wondered Keanyn to himself. *I'd have thought he would have come roaring in with all guns blazing by now.*

Grannison looked at the captain as if he were reading his mind and said, "You expected Ansmed to have immediately attacked us as soon as he got back to his ship."

Keanyn gave a start as Grannison's statement hit him as if his thoughts had been spoken out loud. As he collected himself, he glanced at his second-in-command and said, "As a matter of fact, commander, that is exactly what I expected. Here we sit, prepared to engage a madman bent on blasting us out of the cosmos and he seems in no hurry to do so!"

JA, who was back at his communication station, offered an explanation. "If I may, sir. I think our antagonist is playing mind games with us. By delaying what we fully expected to happen, Ansmed is testing our nerves, hoping that we become less vigilant and drop our guard, ever so slightly. Then he comes in and lowers the boom."

"I think JA is very astute in his thinking, captain," stated Carl Burdgess from his navigator's chair. "It's been over four hours since he 'vanished' from our sights in the mall. More than enough time to have gotten to his ship, prepared it for attack, and launched it toward a confrontation with us."

"That's exactly right!" declared Grannison. "Indeed, it's been plenty of time for us to formulate a plan, get everyone in place, and prepare to meet Ansmed's onslaught. His absence suggests that JA's conclusion is probable."

Keanyn breathed a sigh of resignation. "In a way, Ansmed's delay has given us time to muster up a better defense. Ambassador Calluran successfully convinced the Janovian government and military that sending ships to help defend us is also protection for them." He smiled as he recalled the ambassador's report to them just an hour earlier. He said, "Of course, it helped when he told them that two Janovian scientists helped Ansmed escape from our ship following his murderous attack."

Just then, the lift doors opened and Mac emerged with Edward Butler and Lindsey Thompson in tow.

"Captain!" she said. "Chief Engineer Stokes was indeed correct. He was able to solve the engineering problems that would have kept us from the transport issues we had discussed. And, with Lieutenant Thompson working out the computer glitches, I was able to analyze the physics involved. With zealous encouragement from Lieutenant Commander Butler, I made some slight corrections that solved the equation and made Edward's initial idea doable."

At her mention of the zealous encouragement from Edward, Grannison Loche chuckled knowing how persistent and persuasive his brother could be.

"Well, Lieutenant Commander Stinson, it will please you to know that I have come up with an idea for the use of your successful experiment," declared Keanyn with satisfaction.

Mac and the rest of those who occupied the bridge were waiting to hear the captain's idea but were disappointed when he said, "I will make it known to you after I get the details of Science Officer Stinson's labors. Not everyone here"—he pointed out Stella Steel and Mrs. Pickle along with Saffaw and Salfrod before continuing—"is privy to what we are talking about and will need to be filled in before I can explain."

"What makes you think I'm unaware of what Lieutenant Commander Stinson was working on, captain?" inquired Clarice Pickle.

"I apologize, ma'am," said Keanyn. "I keep forgetting your recently revealed position in the investigative community. I'm sure you are fully informed of our activities."

"Did you tell your aunt?" Robert whispered into ND's ear.

She looked at Robert with a playful grin and answered, "Not about this transporting issue. She's just having fun embarrassing Keanyn, knowing that will allow her to find out a lot sooner."

Robert had the same grin on his face as he said, "No offense, ND, but that old broad is slicker than a greased pole cat."

ND said, "No offense taken. I've been the brunt of her mischief for years. And it sounds as if you've been listening to Captain Paxton's down-home tales again. A greased pole cat?"

Keanyn fidgeted uncomfortably in his command chair before speaking. "Then we will have to have a brief meeting on this matter. Seeing that everyone here is involved, in some way or another in our investigations, I see no need to adjourn to another location in order to meet. That being said, I do need to send some of you on assignments to prepare for whatever Ansmed has up his sleeve."

He sent Saffaw and Clarice to the mall to make sure things had gotten back to normal. Robert was sent to the mall as well to have Ross Carter monitor the Frothy Mug for any transport activity that might occur. He sent Edward and Lindsey back to engineering in case they needed to implement their plan soon and help Stokes with any problems they might encounter with the innovative transporting method.

The remainder of the crew on the bridge either had duties there or needed to be briefed on what Mac and the others had done to the transporting computers and why.

"I can't think of a better way to put the new transporting techniques to use in its initial operation," stated Keanyn after he had explained his idea to everyone.

Mac was the first to express her approval. "I concur, captain. Not that I'm a vengeful person, but it only seems fitting to end things by implementing our discovery in such a fashion . . . if we get the chance."

Stella Steel contributed her thoughts. "I've been shielded off in the mall with all the plants and flowers, but I had several discussions with Mac. So I wasn't totally in the dark about what was going on. But I do wonder. This idea of yours, captain. It seems to me it will need to work almost perfectly if it's going to succeed. The timing alone will prove to be a monumental challenge for something so new and untested."

Salfrod said, "She is speaking for me and, by the looks on their faces, several others on the bridge."

"That includes me," stated Grannison. "Especially when I will be the one piloting this craft during the operation."

Keanyn nodded his acknowledgment of their concerns, saying, "I share your anxiety. But, every new endeavor comes with risks and if we don't try this, we will surely be destroyed by Ansmed's insane aggression. I would rather go out trying to do something to foil his plans than passively wait for our end at his hand. We will make this work!"

All on the bridge nodded their agreement.

CHAPTER THIRTEEN

SHOWDOWN!

"It's been two Earth days since you escaped from their ship," stated Radule Omnivie to Commander Ansmed Kleek. "When do you plan to mount your offensive against them? They don't seem to be in any defensive position as if they were awaiting your attack. Wouldn't now be a good time?"

"That's why you are a diplomat and I am a warrior, Mr. Secretary," noted Ansmed. "You don't attack the moment you think your enemy has let his guard down. You wait a bit longer and let him get a little more anxious. The more nervous he gets, the more likely he is to make mistakes. No, I think I'll give them another day to—how do earthlings put it? Ah, yes—stew in their juices."

"For someone who hates the Earth and its inhabitants, you seem to delight in using their metaphors," Ambassador

Musslavo announced as he entered the guest quarters where Ansmed was staying under the name Nezzaly Dukduk, special envoy for entertainment.

"Since I'm about to wipe them out of existence, I feel that using their own terminology is appropriate," remarked Ansmed with a malicious grin.

Secretary Omnivie gave a slight bow to the ambassador before saying, "Commander Kleek thinks he'll wait another day before he begins his attack on the Earth convoy."

The Ambassador looked intently at Ansmed and said, "You might want to rethink that, commander. I've just come from a summons to a meeting with the premier of Janos. He is very unhappy with our apparent backing of you and your little display on board the *Mall* starship. I assured them that we had no idea of your motives for going on the diplomatic mission and that your actions were the result of a personal vendetta against certain individuals on their ship.

"When they asked if we were aware of your current whereabouts, I replied 'no' but said that we had some ideas we had been exploring. I can't hold them off for long before they come looking for you. I also was informed that Ambassador Calluran had negotiated for their support in case of an attack and were promised several starfighters would come to their aid."

"My uncle wasted little time in showing his true colors," said Ansmed with disgust. "It's a pity he'll have to die with his Earth friends when I blow up their pathetic project! I guess I will have to launch my offensive a half day early." He called all his crewmen to prepare for an attack in ten Earth hours!

Dooley Paxton had been sitting in position for over two days and was beginning to get restless. Inactivity was not something he enjoyed and two days of it was almost more than he could take.

He got on the comm line to the *Mall* ship and keyed in the code for the captain. At Keanyn's acknowledgment, he began to speak, "I reckon he's trying to wait us out to see if we blink first."

Keanyn was used to Dooley ignoring procedure when it came to his friends. He responded to his statement with, "I reckon you're right, my friend. I appreciate you having my back, but, then, you're used to it."

"I've gotten used to your backside. I've come to appreciate that it's your better side," noted Dooley.

"I'll remember that the next time we play 'Alien Roadblock' at the virtual reality gaming complex in the mall. This time, my friend, you're toast!" Keanyn shot back.

Dooley and Keanyn could have continued this banter for hours, but it was Dooley who got serious first. He said, "How much longer do you think that Ansmed fella is going to make us wait, Keanyn?"

Keanyn answered with no little frustration in his voice. "I can't be certain, Dooley. But, if we show that we have slacked off even more in our vigilance, I wouldn't put it past Ansmed to spring his attack before another day is done."

"I certainly hope he does, because I'll be ready for him!"

"I've been in contact with General Beckton on Janos. He's acting as liaison between us and General Monshumahn of the Janovian space force to coordinate our defense against Ansmed's attack," Keanyn informed Dooley. He added, "Ambassador Calluran is working with the pan-global government to deal with the inner-planetary issues between Janos and Saffo V. Since he is also from Saffo V, but also a direct representative of the Legion, he is in an excellent position to keep the Janovian representatives informed of any peculiarities in Saffo Vian negotiations."

Dooley injected a keen observation. "I would imagine that Ambassador Calluran's recent 'stay' in the Saffo V embassy also gives him some clout as one not unduly favoring the negotiating position of the Saffo Vians."

"That does lend weight to his negotiating status, indeed," assured Keanyn. "In view of all these maneuverings, we are as ready for Ansmed as we can be. I'm afraid, old friend, that you will receive the brunt of Ansmed's onslaught since you are the most heavily armed ship he will face. The Janovians can't give us more than a dozen or so starfighters. They have one starcruiser in their dock, but it's being overhauled and would only be at 40 percent weapons capacity even if they could get it launched."

Dooley Paxton was not deterred. "Keanyn, the *Gator* and its twelve tube Stryon torpedo launchers, eight mega laze beam portals, and four hydra-tech cannons will be more than a match for that rebellious coward and his puny starfighter, the *Chicken!*"

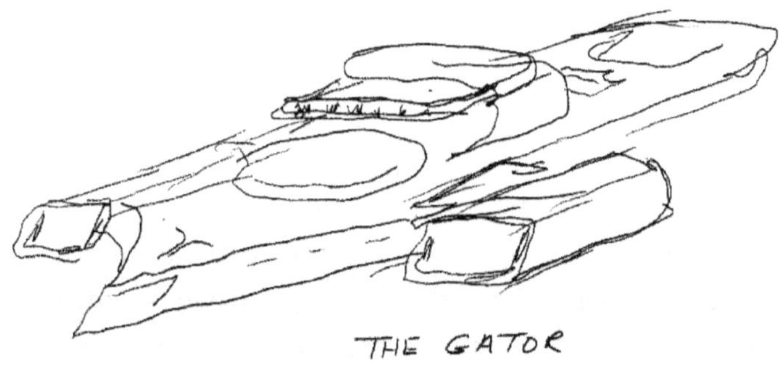

Keanyn smiled broadly at Dooley's purposeful mistake in calling the *Hawk* the *Chicken*, but he warned, "On the surface that seems to be the case, but don't forget that Ansmed outfitted his ship with new state-of-the-art weapons. He also tweaked the engines and modified the design of his ship to make it the fastest, most maneuverable starfighter yet. You may be bigger and more powerful, but he is faster and nimbler. You'll have your work cut out for you."

"We'll see about that, Keanyn," said Dooley. Then he added, "Remember, the proof is in the pudding!"

Just four hours later, JA called Keanyn in his quarters to announce that Ansmed had launched.

Immediately, Keanyn ordered, "General quarters! Prepare for attack!"

When Keanyn arrived on the bridge and sat down at the commander's seat, he immediately checked with engineering to make sure everything was in place for what they had planned. He received a big "all systems go" from Stokes and Mac. She had remained in engineering instead of taking her position on the bridge at the science station in order to oversee the use of the new transporting technique. Lindsey Thompson was right by her side to control the computer operations involved in the new technology. These three would later become known as "the Transporting Triad."

Keanyn next turned his attention to those on the bridge and spoke with confidence and appreciation, saying, "Ladies and gentlemen! We are about to face an unprecedented test of our training and courage. I would like to say I couldn't have more confidence in your abilities than I do right now. But it is your courage in which I have the utmost faith."

"You have shown me, on a number of occasions, that you have applied your training to its highest degree, adding to that your fearlessness in carrying out that training in the most difficult circumstances."

"We are now faced with an attack by a lunatic who is highly armed and dangerous and bent on our destruction. And we have nowhere to run and no weapons to combat his attack. What we do have are the strongest defensive shielding system in the Legion and a ship at our back, commanded by a captain I know will protect us with every weapon he has at his disposal.

"You have all been briefed on our plan. I know, ladies and gentlemen, we will make it work!" Keanyn ordered maximum shields forward and standard shielding around the rest of the ship.

Ansmed came at them, though, from below and hit them with a laze beam strike to the underside of the connecting corridor to the mall. The ship shook and bucked like a bronco, but the shields held.

Next, the Gator came roaring in with six of its Stryon torpedos directed at the *Hawk*.

His shields held as well, but he backed off on any direct attack for the moment, taking stock of what he was up against. His next move was surprising.

"Captain Paxton, the *Hawk* has done a reverse loop and appears to be headed back down to the planet," came word from Dooley's second in command, the Wynrealite, Darmeul Sensa.

Dooley's response was filled with incredulity. "What! A full reverse loop at the speed he was going and at a forty-five-degree ascending angle? That's not possible!"

Commander Sensa said, "Captain Mathews did tell us that Ansmed had equipped his ship with cutting-edge technology. This appears to be some of it."

He looked at his screen as the chief navigator announced, "He's returning at 10 percent light speed in a corkscrew maneuver, firing short blast canon bursts at the *Mall* ship's bridge!"

"Engage with all twelve Stryons," Paxton ordered his weapon's officer, Lieutenant Tom Palmer.

"She's moving too fast in that corkscrew to know whether I'm hitting anything or not, captain," yelled Tom Palmer with frustration. He added, "How can she move like that and still fire?"

"Keanyn warned me this would be difficult," Dooley muttered under his breath. "He's moving like a mad gator."

Then it dawned on him. "He's moving like a gator! I'll fight him like a gator. I can't make the same moves he's making, but I might be able to anticipate where and when he's gonna move."

On the *Mall* ship, Keanyn could only observe as the *Gator* repeatedly tried to zero in on the *Hawk* to get a hit. The infrequent success in that regard left him and the crew feeling helpless. He had feared that all the modifications Ansmed had made to the *Hawk* would prove to be a problem—and it was.

His own ship had received only minor damage, except that he had not expected Ansmed to go after the mall itself so soon.

In the *Hawk's* first pass, directed from underneath the *Mall* starship, Ansmed had made several laze shots on the starboard side of the fuselage where the mall was housed.

Most of the damage there was toppled displays, resulting in mild panic. But the damage to the confidence of the mall employees in the command crew of the ship was greatly damaged.

They were being spared most of the fury of Ansmed's attack because of the relentless attempts of the *Gator* to hammer him with laze beams and Stryon torpedoes, though with very limited success. Dooley's hydra cannons could not be used due to the rapid maneuvering abilities of the *Hawk*.

Keanyn began to notice that the *Gator* was starting to have a little more success at hitting the *Hawk's* shields. He wondered what Dooley had figured out. Still, the best he could hope for was that the shielding on the *Hawk* would be weakened enough to force Ansmed to make a temporary retreat to repair them. He wouldn't quit though. He would simply alter his strategy and return with a better plan. They couldn't settle for retreat. They had to destroy the *Hawk*.

JA suddenly announced, "There are a dozen Janovian starfighters that have just launched from the Eridani Space Station nearby, sir."

Finally, thought Keanyn. *Some ships that can, at least, maneuver like the* Hawk. *They should give Dooley the help he needs to focus his shots more cleanly.*

Keanyn called over to the *Gator* and spoke to Dooley, "Captain Paxton, here comes the cavalry. When they arrive and get in attack position, get into your position so we can begin our plan."

"Thanks for the reminder, Captain Mathews," returned Dooley. "I'm looking forward to seeing how you will pull this off. Here they come, guns a'blazin'!"

As the starfighters arrived, they fanned out in an attempt

to "circle the wagons" around the *Hawk*. Ansmed had other ideas and deftly looped down and around the fighters coming out behind one of them and hitting it with a hyper-blue laser shot. It fanned out, covering it in a magnetic disruption cone that disabled all of the ship's systems, completely crippling it.

Five of the remaining fighters opened fire on the *Hawk*. The other six went above them to come down behind Ansmed. As they did so, the *Gator* moved in from below while the *Hawk* was trapped in the pincer movement. Now, Dooley could finally unload his hydra-tech cannons on the *Hawk*.

Once again, though, Ansmed's nimble little starfighter was able to accelerate instantaneously at a tremendous speed and fly up out of harm's way with barely a chink in its armor.

"What in tarnation has he got in that thing!" exclaimed Dooley, flabbergasted. "I could have sworn we had him dead to rights and he zoomed outta here like a Roman candle!"

Commander Sensa noted, "He's proven to be like a pesky insect that you just can't catch."

"That's true, Darmeul," stated Dooley. "But when you can't swat a fly, you can crush it." He called Keanyn and said, "Are you ready over there, Keanyn?"

"Just been waiting for your word, Dooley," returned Keanyn. "If you can keep him still for just ten seconds, we can do this."

Dooley's reply was firm. "It won't be easy. But sure as a wild gator can be corralled, we'll keep him still."

Keanyn gave the order. "Mr. Burdgess, put us behind the planet and keep us there. Mr. Loche, steer steady with Mr. Burdgess's coordinates. That's the easy part. Getting the coordinates just right for our return will take precision coordination between the two of you and our team in engineering. Are you ready, gentlemen?"

"Aye, Aye, sir!" was said in unison by Grannison and Carl as if they were already synced together.

Keanyn declared, "Then, on my signal, we will move steadily toward Janos's dark side."

As the battle between the *Hawk*, the *Gator*, and the Janovian starfighters raged on, Ansmed failed to notice the departure of the *Mall* ship until his pilot said, "Commander! The *Mall* starship isn't here anymore. It's left the area!"

"Confound all these annoying starfighters!" yelled Ansmed in frustration. "They've kept me from addressing my main goal of destroying the *Mall* ship. Well, they are now going to pay for that."

"Ensign Storuk, load the Kor torpedoes. We're going to blow these pests into the next galaxy! Lieutenant Frenemy, why don't you perform that pirouette maneuver you're so fond of while our weapons officer, Lieutenant Volrum, pops a torpedo into the side of four or five of those Janovian pea shooters."

All of the aforementioned officers gave a resounding aye, aye, and in a matter of minutes, five of the starfighters were destroyed.

The remaining six regrouped and decided to go back to the space station and fight another day, leaving the *Gator* to, once more, face the *Hawk* alone.

On the surface, it looked like an incredible mismatch. A large battle cruiser facing off with a starfighter one-tenth its size. But the *Hawk* had proven to be so elusive with its ultra high-tech maneuverability and quick strike capabilities that it could probably pick apart Dooley's ship piece by piece if given enough time.

Dooley Paxton was aware of all this, but he knew what he needed to do to give Keanyn the chance to make his plan work. He also knew that Captain Keanyn Mathews could make something work when it looked like it was as good as dead. So his money was on Keanyn.

The *Hawk* had started to chase after the retreating starfighters, but only to make sure they were really retreating. Once certain of this, Ansmed turned his nimble starfighter back to where the *Gator* sat waiting for him. He was surprised to see it because he figured that the captain of that ship had realized that, though he had superior firepower, it was useless against the *Hawk's* incredible maneuverability.

"I'll hand it to you, space jockey," said Ansmed to himself. "You get my respect for stubbornness. Despite that, though, I'm still going to have to teach you a lesson that, I'm afraid, you're going to regret."

"What's your plan, captain?" asked Darmeul Sensa back on the *Gator*. "He's coming back and we're the only thing in his way."

Dooley Paxton turned in his command chair to face both Commander Sensa and Lieutenant Tom Palmer and said, "Darmeul, steer us on a path directly at the *Hawk*. Tom, I want you to run a line of Stryons on either side of it. We need to keep that ship from escaping so that it can't run free. Also, run two separate lines of mega lasers above and below him for as long as you can. I'm hoping it will take a minute or two for him to figure out how to escape, as I'm sure he will."

When Ansmed saw that he was boxed in, he slowed his charge to come up with an escape plan. He had come to a near standstill when Dooley radioed to Keanyn the *Hawk's* coordinates on the private ship-to-ship link.

"We've got coordinates, captain!" reported J. A. Philpot excitedly. "Captain Paxton says it's a GO!"

Captain Keanyn Mathews didn't hesitate and checked with Mac in engineering. "Are you ready, Mac?"

"It's all good down here, captain!" she replied.

Keanyn motioned to Stella Steel, who had been sitting quietly at Mac's science station, and said, "Switch on your mic but keep it at mute till I give you the signal." He received a thumbs up. He now gave the order, "Enter the coordinates, Mr. Burdgess. Engage transport, Stokes. And prepare to throttle up, Mr. Loche! We've got a very important engagement to keep!"

Ansmed had just about figured out how to maneuver himself out of his predicament and make the opposing ship pay dearly for its interference. He would unveil his hidden gem. A mini Tragoshun torpedo. It didn't pack quite the wallop of its bigger brother, but it would seriously damage the *Gator's* shields and penetrate enough to cause a major structural breach.

"Commence final preparations for escape and arm the Tragoshun!" ordered Ansmed.

Just then, a voice came through the ship's speakers. It was a female speaking from some unseen location. She said, "This is Stella Steel, Commander Kleek. You killed my friend, Lari. This is for you!"

Suddenly the *Mall* starship appeared, practically filling his view screen. All Ansmed could see was a large metal-like cylinder as it sped toward his ship with no time for any fancy maneuvers.

From the bridge of the *Gator*, the crew watched in gleeful fascination as Keanyn's ship appeared instantly and, using the A deck frontal plate, rammed the *Hawk* at high speed, rendering the fly-like pest nonexistent.

As Ansmed's ship burst into a million pieces, Dooley said, "I told you if you can't swat a fly, you can crush it."

On the *Mall* ship, the impact was barely felt. The cheers, on the other hand, were deafening. When they finally stopped, Keanyn was sitting in the command chair with a satisfied smile on his face. Once again, he rubbed his hands through his disheveled blond hair, breathed a long sigh, and said to his bridge crew, "To say well done seems so insignificant after what we have just accomplished. So, just let me give all of you the most awesome 'WELL DONE' ever!" More cheering followed and Keanyn had no desire to tell them to settle down.

Some five minutes later, Mac, Edward, Lindsey, and Stokes Davis emerged from the lift to more cheers. Mac, humbly, received her congratulations and, as she turned to Keanyn, said, "Captain Mathews, my sincerest congratulations. And, if you don't mind, I would like to perform an act of insubordination."

"That depends on what it is, Lieutenant Commander Stinson," replied Keanyn with all eyes on the two of them.

Mac smiled and walked slowly, but with purpose, to

the command chair and said, as her deep green eyes looked brightly into Keanyn's light blue ones, "Oh. I think you know what it is."

She put her arms around the captain's neck as he gently caressed her face in his hands and the two tenderly kissed for nearly a minute. When they finished, all of the rest on the bridge were smiling. Lindsey Thompson found her voice first and said, "That was the most beautiful kiss I've ever seen."

CHAPTER FOURTEEN

HONORS AND ACKNOWLEDGMENTS

The Janovian Hall of Heroes was certainly the appropriate venue for the joyous assembly that had taken place. The highest dignitaries of both the Janovian military and ruling entities were present along with General Anthony Beckton. Officers and crews of the *Crockett*, the *Gator*, and, of course, the starship *Cosmic Mall* were in attendance as well.

In addition, the arrival of special delegations from the Galactic Legion and Earth added to the importance and uniqueness of the occasion being held.

It was less than an Earth month since the destruction of Ansmed Kleek's ship, the *Hawk*, and Kleek's nefarious attempt to wipe out the mission of the Earth, the *Mall* starship.

This was going to be an evening of bestowing honors to many and acknowledging the contributions of many others.

After acknowledging the roles played by the Janovian military and diplomatic corps, the Grand High Secretary of Janos, Kaldega Stedman III, proclaimed Massnon 44, the Janovian date when Ansmed Kleek's plot had been thwarted, as "Ker Gullapted," or "*Cosmic Mall* Independence Day"!

He continued with his speech, "We have greatly benefited from the *Mall* ship's stay here on Janos. The thought of enjoying the act of shopping has been a revelation to us and has freed us of much stress. We have been told that in many cultures, shopping creates stress. Apparently, these cultures do not know how to shop and interact socially."

There was much humor found in his statement. Especially from earthlings. One from Earth's delegation was heard saying, "Just wait for people to start returning things for cash with no receipt. That's a real hoot."

Shortly after this, the high secretary began honoring the ones directly responsible for the outcome. "First and foremost were Captains Keanyn Mathews and Dooley Paxton. Followed by Lieutenant Commanders MacCardle Stinson and Grannison Loche. While these were in the forefront of the planning and execution of the plans, there were several others who were intricately involved in the outworking of their success. The following is a list of those involved: Stokely Davis, Lindsey Thompson, Cheng Wong, Edward Butler, J. A. Philpott, Carl Burdgess, Robert Porter, Stenn Rotterdam, Natalia Downing, and Clarice Pickle.

"While all of these had a direct hand in either actions that brought about the end result or plans and ideas that were used to bring about the desired results, four names stand out as unexpected. They are; Saffaw, Salfrod, Stella Steel, and Larindo kwark!

"These four had played a role that was either very supportive or crucial to Ansmed's demise. In the case of Larindo kwark, even though she had been a partner with Ansmed, it had been due to the lying propaganda she had been fed by him. In the end, she sacrificed herself for her friend, Stella, when she realized that she had been misled and this action then led to the attack by Ansmed on the *Mall* starship." While the high secretary continued to bestow honors, the speech rambled on for several more minutes.

The next to speak was the head of the Legion's delegation. It was none other than Grand Admiral Haffen Hoo Wangrun. He began with a hearty congratulations from the Galactic Legion for the triumphant success of the Earth's project, the starship *Cosmic Mall*. Not only as a shopping mall in outer space but as the means by which a violent and dangerous enemy of the Legion was eliminated. He then touched on a very interesting subject in quite a peculiar fashion.

"There has been much criticism concerning the choice of a shopping mall as the contribution of Earth for admittance into the Galactic Legion. Indeed, even I and many other high-ranking individuals questioned the choice. Unfortunately, the criticism led to riots, persecution, and murderous violence by those who would stop at nothing to thwart the Earth's project. I am glad that's now behind us!"

He continued on a more positive perspective. "As successful as that project has now become, the Galactic Legion has asked me to officially add to it!"

The audience began to stir excitedly, and none more than those in attendance from Earth.

Admiral Wangrun continued, "During the mission of the

Mall starship, several new and innovative discoveries were made or created. Before this remarkable ship left space dock, the creation of an atmospheric deck was made that revolutionized space entertainment. As if that was not enough, the ability to transport an entire starship from point A to point B was developed. An invention, I might add, that had been attempted many decades ago and several times thereafter to no avail. For these epic accomplishments and others besides, the Legion has decided to add them to your contribution to the Galactic Legion. Earth is now the most highly decorated member of the Legion and has earned a place on the executive counsel."

The hall burst into thunderous shouts, whistles, and applause as the Earth's starship crews received voluminous congratulations and awards from the Legion.

At the end of the speeches and before the entertainment began, it was announced that a Janovian tribunal would begin in two days to make decisions and assess punishment upon the Saffo V embassy and any groups or individuals aligned with them in the heinous conspiracy against the Earth.

It was now a week later, and General Anthony Beckton caressed his gin and tonic as he reclined comfortably in the posh suite of rooms procured for them by the Janovian High Council. He and several of the *Mall* starship's command staff were serving as witnesses in the tribunal the council had convened against the Saffo V embassy.

The embassy's ambassador, its chief secretary, and several of its staff members had been named as defendants. One other was named—Commander Ansmed Kleek was accused of the highest crimes, but he had to be tried posthumously.

General Beckton, along with Captain Keanyn Mathews and several others, were sitting in the suite discussing the day's proceedings.

Lieutenant Commander MacCardle Stinson was sitting next to Keanyn with her head on his shoulder. She said, "It was like our testimony was unnecessary. It was just icing on the cake!"

There were thirteen people in the suite's spacious sitting room. Besides the three already mentioned, they were Grannison Loche, Edward Butler, Robert Porter, and his two cohorts in security, Clarice Pickle, Carl Burdgess, J. A. Philpot, Cheng Wong, and their newest investigative assistant, Stella Steel.

Saffaw and Salfrod would have been there, but Saffaw had been anxious to get back up to the mall and see to the finishing touches being put on the repairs and renovations being made following the *Hawk's* attack on their ship.

As for Salfrod, he had become a close friend to Chief Engineer Stokely Davis since the end of Ansmed's plots, and spent most of his time being schooled by Stokes on the inner workings of the *Mall* starship.

In the courtroom that day, Ambassador Musslavo of Saffo V had tried to give evidence that Ansmed had acted as a loose cannon who was seeking revenge for a personal grudge against the Earth.

"In no way was he acting with the support or blessing of Saffo V or any member of the embassy staff!" Musslavo had vehemently stated.

Then he was asked by the prosecuting attorney in cross-examination, "If Commander Kleek received no support from you or anyone else in the Saffo V Embassy, does that mean he just walked into the embassy, took the keys for a suite of rooms, and made himself at home?"

Even after strong objections from the defense that this called for conjecture on the part of the witness, the chief judge overruled them and ordered Musslavo to answer the question.

Though he refused to do so at first, he was persuaded to respond and said, "I had been expecting my nephew to arrive from Saffo V for a visit and when I saw that the keys were gone, I assumed he had taken them and let himself into the suite."

"If nothing else then, Mr. Ambassador. Wouldn't you call that a major breach of security?" questioned the prosecutor.

When Musslavo remained tight-lipped, the prosecutor turned his back to him and with a dismissive wave of his hand said. "No more questions."

No more were needed. It was clear that the ambassador had dug his own grave and had thrown a considerable amount of dirt on Saffo V as well.

Secretary Omnivie had added a tremendous amount of incrimination to himself and the embassy as well. As he was pulling documents out of his valise to present as evidence to support his claim that Ansmed had acted independently of Saffo V and its embassy, all of the communiques from Larindo kwark came with them and fell on the floor. When the bailiff picked them up and glanced at them, he immediately gave them to the judges.

The prosecutor insisted that they be admitted as evidence and the following testimony of the *Mall* starship's officers was indeed icing on the cake.

Keanyn shook his head in disbelief as he referred to Omnivie's blunder. "I can't believe that numbskull never got rid of such incriminating evidence!"

Stella Steel, who was sitting quite close to Stenn, had an

emotional comment. "I really appreciate how all of you came to the defense of Lari when the tribunal was considering her part in the sabotage and the A deck deaths. Every one of you insisted that she had been brainwashed and coerced by Ansmed and her repentance was underscored by the sacrificing of herself for me. Their decision to name her as merely an unwilling participant whose heroic actions demonstrated her true character gave her an honorable legacy." She finished with tears running down her face.

Stenn reached over and embraced her gently in his arms, which elicited a never before seen response from his mother. ND began crying and leaned across her son to embrace him and Stella.

The room was utterly silent as the occupants were rendered speechless.

Eventually, Clarice spoke, "That's my real niece. Finally showing her true sweet self." But she was also dabbing tears from her eyes.

Keanyn, then made an observation. "The sabotage was included in the tribunal as citizens of Janos had been on the A deck when it shut down and when their own starfighters were fired on. With the loss of life, they had the basis for murder charges as well as clandestine espionage and using Janovian property for criminal activity."

"When their sentence is read tomorrow, it will only be the beginning," stated Cheng Wong. "They will have to be tried for crimes against the Legion. Including treason and rebellion."

Carl Burdgess voiced a comment regarding JA. "You came up with a surprise of your own, JA. How long had you been working on the ability to use voice communication while in transport mode? Having Stella deliver her message to Ansmed while in 'trans mode' completely confused him and gave him no time to react once we popped into view."

JA's answer was, "Once we learned of Edward's idea about transporting the whole ship, I got to thinking about what I might be able to come up with that could complement or enhance it from a communications standpoint. I didn't tell anyone about it because we were all so busy with how to stop Ansmed that I didn't want to burden anyone else with my idea."

"When I finally figured it out, I did enlist Lindsey Thompson's help. I needed her to program my results into the communications computer. I told her not to tell anyone because I wasn't sure how we could use it in dealing with Ansmed. When Keanyn revealed his ramming solution, I figured out how we might use it. When he promised Stella she would be included in the finale, I suggested that we have her send Ansmed that final message."

"That message not only took Ansmed by surprise, but the rest of us as well!" declared Robert.

Keanyn explained, "I thought it would be great theater to spring that on you. Only JA, Lindsey, Stella, and I knew about it. I thought it was a great finishing touch and, while not erasing the loss of her friend, would give Stella some closure."

Stella looked appreciatively at Keanyn and said, "I thank you, once again, for that kindness, captain." Then she turned to Mac and stated, "My old college roommate and I have strengthened our bonds and that has helped with the death of Lari. But I'm not going to be able to get too much of her free time though, as she has found a new interest." She smiled with no hint of regret at having to share her friend.

"Well," said Clarice. "We've got romance in the air since Ansmed is no longer a problem. It appears like my great nephew over there has lost his heart to the charming

Miss Steel in addition to our captain and science officer." She couldn't help stating the obvious when everyone else was trying to be tactfully quiet about it.

Stenn did react to his great aunt's statement. "I was, merely, trying to comfort Miss Steel. As she was upset and I was sitting next to her, I felt it was my duty to ease her emotional distress with a friendly embrace."

The rest of the room's occupants either rolled their eyes, hid smiles behind their hands, or, like Keanyn and Robert, laughed out loud at what they all knew was a load of horse doo-doo. Even Stella smiled coyly and gave Stenn a soft punch on the arm.

"All right! All right!" protested Stenn. "Maybe we do kind of like each other. But she needs somebody right now and I'm happy to be there for her."

ND patted her son's hand and said, "You're a caring person, son. Stella is a fine young woman and she will make you a better man. I don't doubt it."

Grannison observed, "Lindsey isn't with us. I haven't seen her since the tribunal adjourned."

"I forgot to mention," said Cheng Wong. "She and Salfrod left to go to engineering." She had an ornery smile as she said, "I noticed they were walking hand in hand."

The room was now abuzz with voices having three romances to talk about.

Eventually, everyone left except General Beckton, Keanyn, Mac, Grannison, and Robert.

"Robert, I heard you had located a few more of Ansmed's moles on the ship," observed the general.

Robert replied, "Yes, general. Aside from kwark and the two that performed the sabotage, whom we believe were on the *Hawk* when we rammed her, we apprehended three others who had transported to this ship."

"What problems did they pose?" wondered Beckton.

"We've discussed the one who was supposed to sabotage the climate control systems already," stated Keanyn.

"That's right," noted Robert. "But we've recently discovered how he was going to do it in such a way as to make it appear as if the system was at fault and not that it had been tampered with."

"Very interesting, Robert," said Grannison. "I happen to know that the other two moles were planted to undermine the morale of the mall employees so that the service given by them to their customers would be less than acceptable."

Robert nodded and added, "More than that, commander. Those two were also used to help Kleek brainwash Larindo kwark and the eleven other Sharlees to alter their personalities. They were trained as motivational speakers who could motivate negatively as well as positively."

"It seems as if Ansmed Kleek was a psychopathic genius," remarked Keanyn. "He, not only, constructed a violent and murderous sabotage of this vessel, but he was adept at using subtlety as well. He was an extremely dangerous individual!"

Mac spoke with assurance. "And that is why I have no regrets in having had a hand in his destruction!"

Grannison said, "I know that Ambassador Calluran has been greatly affected by his nephew's actions, but he harbors no illusions. He has told me that Ansmed received the punishment he deserved even though he was part of his family."

"That reminds me," noted Keanyn. "Whatever happened to Ansmed's mother?"

Robert replied and there was disgust in his voice. "It seems that Ansmed had been doctoring her food with a drug that brought on insanity. All while appearing to be the loving son who doted on his mother."

"Ambassador Calluran told me that Ansmed's total lack of any kind of love as exhibited in the treatment of his mother, the ambassador's sister, was more reprehensible than his other crimes!" Robert concluded.

General Beckton had a question he had been dying to pose to Keanyn, "Keanyn, using the A deck frontal plate to ram the *Hawk* was dripping with irony, wouldn't you say?"

Mac looked up at Keanyn as she reclined in the comfort of his arms, "I've been meaning to ask you about that as well, love."

Keanyn remarked with mock authority. "That is awfully familiar behavior toward a senior officer, lieutenant commander. It might even be labeled sexual harassment."

"And what do you call holding me in your arms and kissing the top of my head, captain?" countered Mac.

"Protective custody!" returned Keanyn.

After they had all had a good laugh, Grannison turned the conversation back to the previous mention of the A deck. "Captain, when we were trying to figure out how we were going to use the brilliant discovery of transporting the entire ship, why did you decide on using the A deck?"

"Without any offensive weapons whatsoever, the only way we could attack the *Hawk* successfully was to ram it. There was no way we could do that without causing damage to this ship and possible loss of life. I remembered that in the development of the A deck, the engineers used the thought of a battering ram from the old sea battles to give it an added feature. However remote the need for it might be. After the murderous sabotage perpetrated by Ansmed, I was determined to avenge those deaths," stated Keanyn with firm resolve.

General Beckton looked at Keanyn with respect and

said, "I wondered how you would turn out as I followed and occasionally played a part in your life. I saw how well Grannison turned out and knew his father would be proud. But you, Keanyn, were of a different sort. Impetuous, courageous, and unpredictable. Yet able to bring out the best in those around him. If anyone could have come up with a way to take out a heavily armed and incredibly maneuverable spacecraft using a ship with no offensive weapons whatsoever, it was you!"

Grannison Loche added to the thought, "When I first saw that my captain was going to be a kid half my age and fresh out of officer training, I thought that I would have to nurse him through his command. But it shortly became apparent that this young man had what it took for leadership. Yes, he was a bit brash and overconfident, but he became a captain and leader I would follow anywhere."

The room fell silent as the others looked with admiration at Captain Keanyn Mathews. Those looks, quickly, turned to surprise as they saw Keanyn do something unexpected. He was blushing a bright red.

General Beckton swirled the last of his drink in his glass, moved his gaze across the faces of the four others, and said, "Yes, Keanyn, only you would have thought of using the very instrument of Ansmed's treachery to bring justice home to that murderer. The irony is not lost on the rest of us."

Captain Keanyn Mathews found his composure, took a long last drink of his mixed drink and said, "General, whatever do you mean by irony? What irony?"

Acknowledgments

In addition to the wonderful individuals I acknowledged in the first book, *The Earth's Project*, I would like to add the following:

Magie Diaz, who came all the way to my house to get an autographed copy.

The Wilson family and their two boys, Evan and Ashton. These two young men have been very encouraging in not only showing interest in *The Earth's Project*, but contributing their time and effort in helping me market the book. Their parents, Jason and Tracie, are supportive and have trained their sons well.

Liam Schaub is another young man I used to help with audio and visual promotions. The skill he demonstrated was of tremendous quality and made a number of my promotional videos stand out as truly professional. He is also well supported by his parents, Tom and Carmen.

Michael Karvelis who had me on his podcast twice and has contributed some interesting ideas for future projects.

And, lastly, Kevin Bingham whose drawings of the other ships in the *Comic Mall* convoy served as an inspiration.

About the Author

Mr. Tuskey was born in 1951 in Wheeling, West Virginia, to hard-working parents who instilled in him the sound values of that generation. He received a comprehensive spiritual education and taught a public-speaking class for some twenty-five years.

He developed a love of reading in the ninth grade when his English teacher had the class read Dickens's *Great Expectations* and discuss it. His love of literature and his vivid imagination moved him to think about writing a story of his own. After several attempts, it culminated in a dream he had no intention of writing about—until he told his wife about the dream. He now happily lives with her, having been married forty-eight years in the town of Rincon some fifteen miles outside of Savannah, Georgia.